Death By Design
A Josiah Reynolds Mystery

Abigail Keam

Worker Bee Press

Death By Design

ISBN 978 0 9906782 7 4

5 2016

Published in the USA by

Worker Bee Press
P.O. Box 485
Nicholasville, KY 40340

Abigail Keam

Acknowledgements

Thanks to my editor, Faith Freewoman

Artwork by Cricket Press
www.cricket-press.com

Book jacket by Peter Keam
Author's photograph by Peter Keam

Prologue

With a hand clad in a sleek, black leather glove, the intruder punched in the code for the security system and silently slipped into the spacious condo located on the Upper West Side in New York City. Satisfied no one had seen him, or if they had, they would not be able to provide a positive ID, the intruder took his time to peruse the condo, taking care not to disturb anything.

It was crucial no one realize that the intruder was looking for specific items–bits and pieces of precious polished rocks and crystals, small baubles that sparkled in the light and were worth a king's ransom.

In fact, the gems had originally come from an Indian prince, who presented them to his English mistress many years ago, when India was still under the British Raj.

Decades later, when old and infirm, the mistress fearing a robbery, cleverly hid her baubles and died without revealing the secret of their location.

However, the story of the gems didn't die with the old

woman. Generations since had searched for the treasure without success, but Her Ladyship's diary made it clear she had hidden her treasure in plain sight, among her everyday things—but no one had been able to fathom exactly what that meant.

Knowing that the owner of the condo would be out for some time, the intruder took time to carefully examine antique furniture for hidden drawers, as well as searching for wall safes, dusty trunks, examining pockets of old dresses, backs of paintings, and the insides of bric-a-brac. He even searched for mundane collections such as postage stamps. The intruder hadn't watched the classic film *Charade* with Audrey Hepburn and Cary Grant, where a fortune was exchanged for rare stamps, for nothing.

But nothing was all he found—a big fat zero.

The intruder glanced at the clock and knew time was running short. Frustrated, the thief felt he must have actually laid eyes on the treasure, but simply failed to recognize it. Hurriedly, he took pictures with his cell phone until he heard the ancient elevator door whine open on the condo's floor.

Damn it! The owner was back early. Quickly looking around to make sure nothing was out of place, he slipped out the servants' entrance and hurried down the steps to exit via the service elevator, secure in the knowledge that no one would question his casual attire.

Once outside, the intruder sauntered into Central Park and began jogging, knowing full well people seldom took notice of a person exercising in their neighborhood.

Another clean getaway.

The intruder smiled at his escape. He would soon have another chance to re-enter the condo and resume his search. And search he would . . . until he found the treasure.

1

Irvin S. Cobb once said, "To be born in Kentucky is a heritage, to brag about it is a habit, to appreciate it is a virtue."

That's great, but who was Irvin S. Cobb? He was a Kentucky boy who went to New York, and became the highest paid staff reporter in America in the early part of the twentieth century. He wrote sixty books and three hundred short stories, many of them about Kentucky. In fact, he came to be known as a Kentucky writer, even though he spent most of his life in New York City.

It seems you have to live somewhere other than Kentucky to write about it. I wonder if New Yorkers flee New York in order to write about the Big Apple.

That's where I was now–New York.

I found New York is nothing more than a collection of villages jumbled together with no particular rhyme or reason. Still, one does not expect to run into someone she knows back home amidst a collection of villages which are home to over eight million souls. The odds are overwhelmingly against it. Right? So what happened to me had to be fate? Right?

I was strolling down 75th Street on the Upper East Side when I heard someone call my name.

It's hard to stop and turn around on a sidewalk in New York when a gazillion people are tramping in the opposite direction. I thought I was imagining things, but then I heard it again.

"Josiah! JOSIAH REYNOLDS!!"

I ducked into a doorway and cautiously peered around a column. There did indeed appear to be a rotund lady wrapped in a beige cashmere coat with matching leopard printed hat and gloves, hoofing to where I was hiding–I mean waiting. Okay. I was hiding.

Out of breath, she started to go into the building under whose portico I had taken refuge, when she spied me behind the marble edifice. "Josiah Reynolds. I thought that was you. Then I thought, no, it couldn't be. June told me you were visiting New York, and that I should call you, and that's exactly what I was going to do this afternoon, but then poof–there you were, right in front of me. I never thought my luck could be that good." She peered closely at me. "You are Josiah Reynolds, are you not, the woman who lives next door to

Lady Elsmere? I was tempted to call you Josie. Josiah's such an unusual name for a female."

"And you are?" I asked. Hey, I wasn't going to admit who I was. This woman could be a bill collector or a hit man for all I knew.

Don't jump to conclusions. I am not paranoid.

"I'm Bunny Witt of the Philadelphia Witts, not to be confused with the Boston Whitts. They spell their name differently, with a h."

"Unhuh," I murmured. "And why is Bunny Witt of the Philadelphia Witts calling my name on 75th Street?"

"I'm no longer of the Philadelphia Witts. I live in New York now, when I'm not in Kentucky for the racing season, or if I'm not in Florida, you know, for the winter. I can't abide those frigid winters in New York and Kentucky anymore. I have to have the warmth for my feet, you know."

"No, I didn't know," I muttered, watching Bunny Witt's hands flutter about her face like an injured bird trying to take flight.

"I was just going to call June and ask for your number when I looked up–and there you were. It's amazing. I prayed about this, you know, only last night, but seeing you the next day, I mean, I didn't think God produced results that fast."

I interrupted, "Mrs. Witt, I'm very sorry, but I have no idea what you're talking about."

"Of course not. I haven't explained my problem yet, have I? But I so desperately need your help." She clutched my hand that wasn't holding the cane . . . you know, the cane with the silver wolf's head. "Please say you will help me. You simply must."

Finally aware of the befuddled expression I was displaying, she pulled on my arm. "The Carlyle Hotel is just around the corner. Let me buy you a drink at Bemelmans Bar and I can explain my predicament." She gave my arm a little tug. "Just give me twenty minutes. Please."

"You buying?"

"Assuredly."

"In that case, you can have twenty-two minutes of my time."

The anguish in Bunny's face eased a bit and she smiled. "I've heard that you have a quick tongue."

"New York brings out the Dorothy Parker in me. If you thought that was witty, you should see me after three drinks. I'm more Oscar Levant than Oscar Levant."

Bunny's face went blank. "I don't mean to sound obtuse, but I have no idea of whom you are speaking. Do the Levants own a horse farm in Lexington?"

I started to whip out a sarcastic barb, but why waste my considerable talent on this harebrained tootsie? Should I squander time explaining that Oscar Levant was one of the great scathing wits of the twentieth century? No, I would keep my quips to myself until someone worthy came along. Right now my leg was hurting, and I needed to sit down. To tell the truth, my dogs were barking, so Bemelmans Bar sounded just fine and dandy, especially if the drinks were free.

2

I ordered pink champagne while Bunny ordered white wine. We sat in a dark corner of Bemelmans Bar. I chose a seat with my back to the wall so I could see all the exits. Not that I'm paranoid. No—not me. Quit thinking such things.

The bar was named after Ludwig Bemelmans, the creator of the popular Madeline children's books, who painted delightful murals of picnicking bunnies and ice-skating elephants in exchange for free lodging for his family. The murals gave the bar a whimsical ambience. Who could resist pictures of children and bunnies in suits frolicking in Central Park, especially while systemically getting soused?

"Bunny. May I call you Bunny?"

Bunny nodded while grabbing some nuts from a dish on the table to munch on.

"Uh, Bunny, surely you realize that I had a severe accident over two years ago."

"Oh yes, it made all the papers. June was beside herself. She thought you were going to die. She didn't like that. Not at all. She said to me, 'What will I do for amusement without my Jo?'"

I nodded, as this was my intro. "I didn't like it myself. However, because of the accident, I don't remember things as well as I should. Sooooo, I must confess I don't remember you. Obviously, you know Lady Elsmere, but my question is still–who are you?"

Bunny looked startled. "Oh, I don't know what to say. I didn't realize. I mean, the last time we met we had such a good dialogue. I should apologize for not introducing myself, or at least say I'm sorry for your disability. June never divulged that you had memory problems. If she had, I never would have said boo to you. I didn't know. Of course, I would have said hello when I saw you on the street, but I never would have burdened you with my problems."

I was growing very irritated with Miss Bunny's rambling. "Just who the hell are you?" I snapped, cutting to the chase.

Bunny nervously glanced around to see if anyone had heard my outburst. "I'm Bunny Witt of the Philadelphia Witts, without the h."

"I got that."

"I met you at several of Lady Elsmere's parties. We talked about her new portrait where she posed like Queen Elizabeth by William Dargie."

I shrugged.

"We met again at June's private box at Keeneland. My horse came in second, just behind her Jean Harlow. My husband threw bourbon in our trainer's face. He was my husband then, but he's not now. June ordered him out of the box, and he fell over your cane. He threatened to sue you, saying you had tripped him on purpose."

Knowing me, I probably had.

Suddenly a light bulb went on in my head. "That ass was your husband? What a waste of good bourbon!"

Bunny looked apologetic. "As I said, he's not my husband now. We've been divorced over six months. He embarrassed me so much I just had to get rid of him. A nasty temper there, and I've got to tell you, he cost me a pretty penny and . . ."

I interrupted again. "Bunny, I remember now. Why do you need to talk with me so urgently? Does it have to do with your ex-husband?"

Bunny looked panicked. "Oh, no, it has nothing to do with him. He's gone. I paid him a lot of money to get gone and stay that way. I never liked him much anyway. Such a bully."

"Please get to the point, Bunny."

"Yes. Yes. To the point. Josiah," she said, laying her hand on my arm, which kept me from taking a much-needed swig of my pink champagne. What was the point of getting a free cocktail if one couldn't drink it? I wanted to shake her hand off, but she hung on to me like a tick on a hound. She looked around and then leaned toward me. "I think someone is stalking me."

"You think? You don't know?"

Suddenly Bunny seemed frightened. "I have an apartment here in New York, and one in London. You don't know this about me, but I'm very OCD. Everything has to be in its place. It has to do with my rigid upbringing by a German governess. Personally, I think she was a former Nazi the way she . . ."

"Does your Nazi governess have anything to do with the stalking?"

"No. She's dead, thank goodness."

"Okay, let's skip the childhood reminiscences and get straight to why you think you are being stalked."

"In both my London and New York apartments, I feel like someone has, on several occasions, entered and gone through my things. London was the worst. Yes, London was very bad."

"Was anything taken?"

"Nothing, but certain things had been moved."

Bunny was gaining my attention now. I leaned forward in my chair, removed her hand from my arm, and took a sip of my champagne. "How had things been moved?"

"Items only I would notice. Like I said, I'm very OCD. I line my hairbrush up with my comb very precisely. Several times I have found my brush tilted, not straight."

"Maybe your cat jumped up on your dresser."

"I don't have a cat. I know you think I'm being silly, but that's just one item I've noticed."

"Dish."

"I'm very particular about my clothes. On several occasions, I've noticed a number of my blouses turned the wrong way. I face all my coats, blouses, shirts, and jackets to the left. It looked like a few blouses had fallen and someone put them back on the hanger but facing right. I know it sounds crazy, but someone has been in my apartments."

Bunny had my attention. She was neurotic, but not stupid, and obviously very observant.

"Anything else?"

"Several times I have felt as though someone was watching me. I once saw a man standing at a bar in a restaurant who seemed to be studying me. At least that's what I thought."

"Can you describe this man?"

"No. By the time I gathered my courage to confront him, he was gone. Then another time, I happened to glance out my living room window and I thought I saw a similar man across the street looking up at my windows. When he saw me, he walked away. It just gave me the creeps."

"You should call the police."

"To say what? That my blouses were turned the wrong way in my closet, and I think I saw a man staring at me from the sidewalk? I can't even describe him, except that he was white. He was in the shadows both times."

"Why are you sharing this with me?

"I called June to tell her what was happening, and she suggested I talk to you since you were in New York."

"I'm just here for a few days before I head back to Lexington. I don't know how I can help you. Perhaps you need to hire a detective."

"Can you please come by and just look at my apartment? I went out this morning and when I came back, some more of my things had been moved. I want you to see it. I was so frightened I ran out of the apartment, and was going to a friend's house when I saw you on the street by accident. But it couldn't have been an accident, could it? I think I was meant to run into you."

In defiance of my doctor's orders, I had drunk two champagne cocktails, and was feeling pretty loosey-goosey. Sure, why not? I had nothing important to do. "Where's your apartment? I can't walk very far."

Bunny's face brightened. "Let me pay the waiter and then I'll get a cab. I live on the west side."

Seemed okay to me. But while she went outside to get a cab, I made a quick call to my old friend, June, aka Lady Elsmere, just to see if Bunny Witt of the Philadelphia Witts was on the up-and-up and *thank* her for taking the liberty of offering my services to one of her harebrained friends.

Now I mean it. Quit thinking that. I'm really not paranoid.

3

"You live at the Dakota?" I asked incredulously as I stepped out of the cab and onto the sidewalk with the assistance of the Dakota doorman. Looking around, I muttered, "This is where John Lennon was killed."

"Who?" asked Bunny while paying the cab driver.

"You know, John Lennon. One of the Liverpool Lads."

Bunny's expression remained blank.

"John Lennon was shot right here four times in the back by Mark Chapman. Right here. John Lennon. One of the Beatles."

"Oh, the Beatles. That was before my time." Bunny smirked.

"Well, I didn't realize I'm such an old fart. You do know the movie *Rosemary's Baby* was filmed here?"

"I remember reading something about that."

"Haven't you ever seen it?"

"I don't watch TV or read much. Don't have time."

What little respect I had for Bunny took a nose dive, and I hadn't had much to begin with, but I wasn't going to pass up an opportunity to see the inside of the Dakota. So I meekly followed her through the massive portico and into the courtyard to the elevators. We got on one.

My heart started racing. When the elevator door opened, would I see Ruth Gordon standing there with a glass of herbal tea . . . or maybe the Trench sisters going to the basement, where they killed and cannibalized children from the apartment building?

The door opened.

I drew a breath. No one was there.

Bunny walked off.

I poked my head out, looking back and forth. No Ruth Gordon. No Trench sisters. Such a disappointment. The hallway looked normal, even inviting.

Bunny walked over to a door a few feet away. "I'm very lucky to have an apartment overlooking Central Park," she purred.

I followed Bunny, looking behind me several times, just to make sure no one was there.

Stop that grinning. I AM NOT PARANOID!

We entered a bright, modern-looking apartment with cheerful paintings on the walls and artfully arranged, neutral-colored furniture. What can I say? Bunny had expensive taste. And her expensive taste was really, really boring. Yawn.

I followed her into the master bedroom. She showed me the cavernous chamber that served as her closet. Jeez, I could fit my entire master bathroom and walk-in closet into hers. I had no idea one person could own so many pairs of shoes.

I personally owned two pairs of good shoes to wear with nice outfits, one pair of high heels which I never wear anymore but refuse to throw out (hope springs eternal), one pair of winter boots, one pair of really good walking shoes, one pair of farm boots, and various pairs of shabby flip-flops. This worked out to a total of ten pairs of shoes, not counting bedroom slippers.

"See here. See how the blouses are hanging backwards?"

I peered closely. Sure enough, there were two blouses with the fronts facing right instead of left.

"Who has access to your apartment?" I asked.

"I have a personal assistant and a part-time cook."

"They have keys to the apartment?"

"Only my assistant does."

"How does the cook get in?"

"She always works the same days as the assistant."

"Which are?"

"Every Monday, Wednesday, and Friday."

"And the cook can only get in via the assistant?"

"Yes."

"Who else?" I asked, taking a small flashlight out of my purse. Of course I carry a flashlight in my purse. One never knows when she will need one. "Relatives, Dakota maintenance people?"

"Of course, the building super has keys for the maintenance people, but I have to be notified before they enter the apartment," replied Bunny, watching me turn on the flashlight and peer at the carpet.

"Relatives?"

"No one else."

"How do you receive visitors? Do they just come up?"

"They usually make an appointment with my assistant, or the doorman calls to get permission to allow them inside the building."

"Is the cook or assistant pissed off at you for any reason?"

Bunny looked astonished. "Goodness, no."

I gave her an appraising eye. "No tiffs at all?"

"My assistant has been with me for years and the cook worked for my mother. They are not part of this. They would have no reason to be."

"When you travel, who looks after the apartment?" I asked, gawking through her expensive garments. It appeared Miss Bunny was a bit of a clothes horse.

"The building super. My assistant usually travels with me."

"Where is she now?"

"This is her day off."

"What about the ex-husband?"

"I had the locks changed after he moved out, and all the people at my residences have been instructed not to let him in again."

"Good girl. So many women don't get the locks changed when love goes bad. It proves to be a fatal mistake sometimes."

Bunny nodded. So she wasn't so dumb after all.

"What about boyfriends? Current or exes?"

"I'm not seeing anyone at the moment. No one from my past could get in, even if they had a duplicate key from an earlier time."

I clucked in approval.

"What about the relatives of the help?"

"The cook is a widow who has a successful son in the theater."

I cut in, "If he's so successful, why is his mother still working for you?"

"As I told you, Josiah, she's a widow, and she likes to cook. It gives her something to do, and she's been with my family for two generations now. She's like a second mother to me."

"And the assistant?"

"She has no kin that I know of. I wish you'd get off this train of thought. My employees have nothing to do with this."

"I know. I know. The mysterious man in the

shadows. Has anyone been in your apartment in the past two days?" I asked as I moved around the closet, flashing my light here and there.

"Today is Saturday, so my employees were here yesterday."

"And when was the carpet last vacuumed in here?"

"Yesterday. My assistant vacuumed my bedroom and closet right before she left."

"And no one but you has been here since then?"

"NO!"

I flashed the light over to a corner of the closet. "I believe you, Bunny. If you walk carefully over to where my light is pointing, you will see the partial imprint of a man's running shoe in the carpet." I looked around and saw only two pairs of tennis shoes that belonged to Bunny. I pulled them from their slots and turned them over, checking the tread marks. "None of your athletic wear matches the tread, and look at this." I bent over as much as I could, placing one of Bunny's shoes next to the imprint. It dwarfed Bunny's shoe. "Whoever was in here was tall."

"I'm frightened. What do they want? Nothing is missing."

"Could be some freak with a shoe fetish. I would advise you to have the apartment professionally swept for listening devices and hidden cameras. Then I would suggest you have cameras installed. After all, you're rich. Kidnapping is not out of the question," I said.

Bunny looked aghast at this suggestion. "I don't want to stay here tonight."

"I think you should stay with a friend until you get security beefed up."

"When are you leaving for Kentucky?" asked Bunny.

"I'll be flying out in two days. I am loaning two Roberto Capucci dresses for a fashion exhibit in Lexington, and I have to get them ready."

"Really! So am I. I've got several dresses in the exhibit." Bunny pulled out several Halston and Charles James dresses. "What do you think?"

I gingerly felt the crepe of the James dress. "I've only seen a Charles James in pictures. This is beautiful."

"These are the rejects. I've already sent fifteen dresses to be in the exhibit. I'm flying out as well in a couple of days. We might be on the same plane."

"Oh, goodie," I replied. If Bunny caught any sarcasm in my tone, she ignored it. "Will you wait while I pack a bag and walk out with me? I don't want to be here alone."

I shook my head. "No overnight bags. If someone is watching, you don't want to let them know you're leaving. Borrow stuff from your friend. Just take what cash, medicine, or documents you'll need. Let's try to give whoever is watching the slip. I'll be waiting in the living room."

Bunny didn't look totally convinced, but she did as I directed.

While I waited in the living room, I took the opportunity to sit down. My legs were turning to jelly, but my mind was turning facts over fast, so I turned on a lamp and went through her mail to see if there was anything unusual like hate mail. Nothing. I then studied the locks on her front door. Good, sturdy deadbolts. Nothing looked forced, but Bunny had an old security system that even I could disable.

Twenty minutes later Bunny came out of the bedroom with an enormous Dooney and Bourke handbag.

"Whatever important items you are not taking should be in a safe or better yet a safe deposit box."

"Anything like that is already in my safe."

"Who has the combination?"

"Just me."

"Did you call anyone?"

"No."

"Not even your assistant?"

"No one."

"Okay. Let's see how long it takes your stalker to figure out that you've left New York. Just leave a note for your employees that you're staying with a friend and that you'll be in touch. Don't mention where you'll be staying. You should also have all your phone numbers changed before you leave for Kentucky. In fact, I think you should leave your cell phone here and purchase a new one. I understand a person can be tracked through their cell phone."

Bunny pulled a cell phone out of her bag and left it inside a desk drawer. "What about the doorman?"

"Leave that to me." I replied. "Is there a service elevator?"

"On the other side of the building."

"What about stairs?"

"The same."

"Let's walk down a flight and then catch the service elevator. This is Saturday, so no one should be using it."

I escorted Bunny down the hall to the stairs, and we silently entered the staircase to go down one flight. Then we entered the third floor hall and made our way to the service elevator without anyone seeing us—or so I hoped.

Once outside, we took several cabs to make sure we weren't followed, going downtown and then doubling back uptown to her friend's address. Her girlfriend was waiting on the sidewalk and escorted Bunny inside the building.

After that, I made my way to Asa's (my daughter) apartment, hoping I had seen the last of Miss Bunny of the Philadelphia Witts—not the Boston Whitts.

4

My name is Josiah Reynolds. And, before you ask, my grandmother had a thing for giving the females in the family Old Testament names. I'm an art history professor by education and a beekeeper by necessity.

Truth be told, I'm not a nice person. Oh, I rarely set out to hurt anyone. I don't like cruelty, but if you try to hurt me, I'll cut you.

I used to be soft. I'm not now. It's a crazy world, and I try to skin it any way I can. I've stopped trying to save the planet. I just want to hang on to what I've got and everyone else can just go to hell.

Sound bitter? Yeah, you can say that. You know my story, but here's one new tidbit. I had just left an appointment with a specialist in New York when I ran into Bunny Witt. It seems my kidneys are starting to go on the blink.

Thanks so much, Tellie Pidgeon. You started my rotten tale of woe. Because you bumped off your husband and tried to pin it on me, it allowed Fred O'nan, a crooked cop, into my life, and what a crappy ride it's been since then.

They're dead now. Both Tellie Pidgeon's husband and Fred O'nan. They were taking up space anyway as far as I was concerned.

But O'nan didn't die soon enough. He pulled me off an eighty-foot cliff. I fell forty feet before I hit a ledge. It's been a long climb back up the cliff metaphorically, trying to get my body back into some semblance of normalcy.

Now the docs tell me my kidneys are on their way to bye-bye land. I was warned this might happen, but I never thought it would. Now I have to face the music.

Ah, Jumping Jehosaphat! In other words–ah, shit!!!

But the crap, no pun intended, doesn't stop there.

Before O'nan was killed and swept over the deadly falls of the Cumberland River, he shot Matt, my best friend, before trying to drown me.

Matt has been in Los Angeles recuperating while waiting for his baby to be foaled out of dam, Meriah Caldwell, the famous mystery writer.

So when I got the call from Matt that he was finally coming home to Kentucky with his new baby, I leapt for joy–not really–since I can barely walk sometimes, but in my heart.

Finally, the appointed day arrived for Matt to fly into the Bluegrass Airport.

My pal and Matt's ex-boyfriend Franklin stood beside me wearing a fringed leather jacket, and clutching an enormous bouquet of flowers while we waited for the plane to land.

I guess I should explain that Matt was with Franklin and then broke up with him after Matt fell in love with Meriah Caldwell. (Yeah, Matt swings like a pendulum, whereas Franklin is on the gay and narrow path.) Things went as far as Matt and Meriah getting married, when Lacey Bridges entered the church and shot Doreen Doris Mayfield DeWitt in revenge for Doreen murdering her husband, Addison DeWitt, who also happened to be Lacey's boyfriend. Still with me?

Then, to make things worse, Lacey killed herself as well. Needless to say that put a damper on proceeding with the wedding. It's difficult to say your "I do's" when flicking brain matter off your wedding dress.

After that debacle, it's not clear who broke up with whom. Sometimes Matt says it was Meriah, and other times he says it was his doing.

All I know is Meriah hightailed it back to California with her tail tucked between her legs, a head full of mixed memories, and pregnant.

I never cared for Meriah, but I will say that when Matt got hurt, she pulled out all the stops for him. Meriah had Matt flown to Los Angeles and nursed him back to health while paying all the medical bills.

I guess they couldn't work things out, since Matt was returning to Kentucky with his newborn—a baby girl.

I had hoped Franklin and Matt could repair their

relationship, and naively assumed things would be on the upswing now. Boy, was I wrong.

5

I gave Franklin a once-over. "Trying out for a part in *Seven Brides for Seven Brothers*?"

He gave me a sour look.

"Rodeo in town?" I continued. I was on a roll.

Franklin feigned conspicuous interest in the fringe on his jacket.

"Casting call for a remake of *High Noon*?" I glanced down at his canvas shoes. "What—no cowboy boots?"

Franklin looked the other way.

I sang, "I've got spurs that jingle, jangle, jingle . . ."

"I'm not listening to you," interrupted Franklin, walking away.

"Going to a square dance? No? I hear the '60s calling. They want their fringe back."

"It's pure vintage and cost me a bundle. I see you dressed up a bit yourself. Black pantsuit with a silver blouse. Nice accessories. You've even got on a decent pair of black shoes. Do you have on a pair of granny panties without rips in them?"

"Donna Karan, if you please. I got the outfit in New York, and my undies are none of your business."

"Ooh, hoity-toity. You splurged on a rich bitch outfit. I hope you're wearing a bra without gravy stains."

"I've got on a nice suit that camouflages my flaws instead of shouting them out like that Daniel Boone jacket you've got on."

"That's where you've gone wrong, dearie. I don't have any physical flaws," smirked Franklin.

"HA!" I shot back.

"That's your comeback–ha?"

"I know it's lame, but I'm nervous. Matt's return has me rattled."

"I am too, but everything is ready. I've been over that shed you call a house with a fine-tooth comb, and not a thing is out of place."

"Did you put the handicapped bars up in the bathroom?" I asked.

"Yep."

"Especially the shower?"

Franklin gave me a stony look. "Of course."

"Babyproof the electrical outlets and the bottom cabinets?"

"Done, done, and done. Charles went through the house with me and double-checked."

I turned and waved to Charles, Lady Elsmere's butler and heir, who was waiting patiently with our mini caravan of vehicles.

Lady Elsmere, aka June Webster from Monkey's Eyebrow, Kentucky, had insisted on sending her Bentley for Matt, plus a Land Rover as big as a battleship to carry his things.

Charles nodded and waved back. I could tell he was excited too.

I turned back and saw a private jet touch down on the runway and taxi the tarmac in front of where we were waiting. I grabbed Franklin's arm. "This may be him."

We both waited anxiously as the plane glided to a smooth stop just yards from our little entourage. After a few minutes, the door opened and the stairs unfolded.

A flight attendant peered out, saw us, and pulled back inside. We waited a few more minutes. My left leg was starting to tremble, because I had been standing too long. Matt or no Matt, I was going to have to sit down soon.

An airport worker jaunted over from a nearby building and began unloading the plane's baggage compartment. He pulled out five bags.

That's all? A mother takes more than that for a stroll around the neighborhood.

Finally, a woman emerged with a tiny bundle in her

arms—a bundle that was crying. Babies do not like air pressure changes inside airplanes. Good! The baby's lungs and hearing worked. Now I just hoped she had ten toes and ten fingers.

Franklin emitted a little cry of his own. "Come on," he called to me, as he rushed the stairs in anticipation.

"Give them some breathing room, Franklin," I admonished.

I didn't know what to expect, so I hung back. Franklin had gone to California several times to see Matt, but I had not. A two-hour plane ride to New York was all I could handle. A trans-continental flight was out of the question.

I hadn't seen Matt since I put him on a private plane and dispatched him to the loving arms of Meriah in California. I didn't know what to expect.

A beaming Franklin escorted the woman who was a nurse, and the baby to the Bentley.

Charles and another employee gathered the bags and put them in the Land Rover.

At last Matt emerged, but not the vital, athletic Matt I remembered. This man was wan and gaunt. His clothes hung loosely on his skeletal frame. Matt's beautiful raven hair had lost its luster, and his once-pouty lips were no longer plump and inviting. They were thin and cruelly set. His hands trembled a bit as he tentatively took each step of the stairway.

"Don't you cry, girl," I whispered to myself. "Don't

you dare cry." I pinched myself, forcing a smile while looking up at Matt as he descended.

When Matt got closer, I could see that his blue eyes still smoldered, but the mischievousness was gone.

I thought of the poet Lord Byron, whose illness created a wasted beauty of a most haunting kind.

Matt's restless eyes lighted on me. "Hello, Rennie," said Matt, using his pet name for me. "Good of you to come." He smiled and held out his arms.

I rushed to Matt and buried my face against his chest. I could hear his heart beat. "Matt, my Matt! Ready to go home?" I looked up at him.

His reply was a weak nod.

I noticed that his eyes were moist.

Charles hurried over and excused the flight attendants. The two of us carefully eased Matt into the lush backseat of the Bentley. Franklin had already entered the back from the other side with the baby and the nurse, so I rode shotgun.

During the ride home, I stole glances in the rearview mirror, and always Matt was staring at the back of my head.

Did he blame me for his present condition?

Of course he did.

But hadn't I warned him to stay away from me? Hadn't I begged him to live in the city? Hadn't I told him that living close to me was dangerous? Hadn't he said he would see it through to the end, meaning my situation with Fred O'nan?

Quit making excuses, Josiah, I scolded myself. *You should have pulled him by the hair of the head out of that shed and into town and never seen him again. Look where your selfishness has gotten him.*

Oh, my darling boy. What have I done to you!

6

We all kept our distance and gave Matt several days to settle in without descending upon him.

Lady Elsmere made the first move. She summoned him to a family dinner, including the nurse and the baby. Matt knew Lady Elsmere well enough to realize that declining the invitation was simply not an option.

It turned out to be quite a happy affair. Franklin, Matt, June, Charles and his wife Mrs. Dupuy, their daughters Amelia and Bess, Michael Connor, who brought Shaneika along, (hmm, seems like they are a "thing" now), myself, Matt's nurse, and the baby who was passed around like a sack of potatoes with everyone kissing her cheeks and straightening her hair bows.

Fortunately, she was a good-natured baby and seemed

to thrive on adoration–just like her daddy. The apple certainly hadn't fallen far from the tree in that respect.

It was obvious Matt was a devoted, doting father, beaming whenever the baby gurgled or pooped.

As luck would have it, the nurse got the baby to take a nap so we could enjoy our meal without the gurgling or pooping. I'm not a big fan of either–whether from a baby or an adult for that matter.

June's massive dining room table was laid out for what she considered a casual dinner with her "everyday" china and mason jars for the drinks; the invited wore casual clothes since they knew their shirts would likely be stained with butter, sauce, and grease drippings. Sounds like a typical Southern feast to me!

We had gathered in the library for the customary pre-dinner bourbon cocktails when Charles appeared at the door and announced, "Dinner is served, y'all."

We rushed to the dining room like a passel of ravenous, feral pigs. I nudged Franklin out of the seat I wanted. I like sitting in the middle of the action, where I can see and hear everything. June anchored one end of the table, and Charles, as heir to June's estate, sat at the other. Matt sat on the right of June and next to Amelia.

Amelia had already announced that Matt was too thin, and it was her God-given duty to fatten him up. Whenever Matt looked away, she plopped more potato salad onto his already-laden plate. It was not clear whether Matt noticed his plate was being surreptitiously filled. Nevertheless, he kept eating like some half-starved dog.

Dinner consisted of barbeque slathered in a secret bourbon honey sauce, homemade potato salad, fried green tomatoes, coleslaw, greasy green beans with chunks of salty ham hock, sautéed red beets, an old-fashioned ring mold of cherry Jell-O with bananas, sliced red tomatoes, spicy deviled eggs, corn bread and yeast rolls with honey butter, sweet iced tea, hand-squeezed lemonade, and topped off with Bess' fabulous black walnut cake with hand-cranked pawpaw ice cream.

Since Charles' grandsons, in their teens and early twenties, were still at the atrocious table manners stage, we made them eat in the kitchen. That way they could eat with their hands, or whatever, and we didn't have to see the mess. Silverware be damned! Charles bribed his grandsons with fifty dollars each if they would serve and clean up, so they didn't mind.

Everyone ate with relish.

Matt closed his eyes and savored a bite of green beans. "I've missed Miss Bess' cooking so much. In California, all the food is so trendy and healthy, it's boring."

"Are you saying my food is not healthy?" accused Bess, taking offense. "Most of the food on this table was raised on this farm. Totally organic, and I cooked everything myself."

"No, Miss Bess, what I'm saying is that compared to good Southern cooking, California food is not even food–well, it's cardboard. The only local food in southern California with any taste is Hispanic."

"Don't let some snotty celebrity chef hear you say that. You might get sued," chimed in Franklin.

"Sir, remember you were recuperating. You could only eat bland food," offered the nurse while clearly calculating the fat and salt grams on her plate. It was causing her some concern. She continued, "You couldn't get out to our fine restaurants."

Matt winced. "Again, please call me Matt. Sir sounds like you're addressing my father."

Franklin piped up, "You can call me sir."

The nurse scowled at Franklin. Apparently they had already butted heads about who was running Matt's household.

Miss June pushed her chair back. "I'm so stuffed you're going to have to use a crane to get me to the second floor. Children, as much as I want to talk some more, these old bones need to lie down a bit. Please carry on."

Amelia, who acted as June's caregiver, rose from the table. "Let me escort you, Lady Elsmere, to your room."

June gave everyone a mischievous look. "She calls me Lady Elsmere in public, but in private she calls me 'Old Buzzard.'"

"I do not," protested Amelia. "The awful things you say, old woman."

June grinned. "See?" She rested her hand on Amelia's outstretched arm and let Amelia escort her out of the room.

When he was sure Amelia and June were out of earshot, Matt commented, "June seems quite a bit more frail than when I last saw her."

Charles nodded while he folded his napkin. "She'll be eighty-nine in a few weeks. Her birthday will coincide with the upcoming couture exhibit. She has forty dresses in it. Selecting and cataloging the dresses for the exhibit simply wore her out."

Mrs. Dupuy added, "Exquisite dresses. Some of them are vintage couture from the forties. We had to get most of them out of storage in the attic. You've never seen such lovely clothes."

Franklin added, "Josiah has dresses in the exhibit also."

"I have two, but Shaneika has loaned more than fifteen," I said. "Of course she won't tell us how she managed to acquire her treasure trove of vintage couture."

Shaneika sneered. "None of your beeswax, Josiah. I wish you'd quit pressing me about my background."

"Is there something embarrassing about your background?" inquired Franklin.

"You know how gossip is in a Southern town. If you're black and have a single drop of white blood, everyone wants to know the dirty details. Well, I refuse to descend into the gutter to satisfy people's prurient curiosity."

"Are there dirty details? Is there a gutter to lie in?" pushed Franklin, buttering another roll.

"Franklin, let it slide, boy," warned Michael.

"Just wondering. That's all. Shaneika is always so

evasive about her past and just who her ancestors are. I'm just wondering why all the hush-hush?"

"I'm not hush-hush, Franklin. Why is everyone so interested in my family's history? Let's talk about your family, Franklin. Any dirt there?"

Franklin looked disappointed. "Unfortunately, no. My family is so vanilla, we make Andy and Opie look like drug dealers. The only scandal in my family is me."

"You mean because you're gay?" Charles asked.

Franklin laughed. "No, the fact that I didn't become a doctor like my father. The last three generations of males have been doctors. I majored in computer science. It broke my father's heart."

I changed the subject. "Matt, what's the news with Meriah? Will she be paying us a visit soon?"

Matt folded his napkin, taking his time. I could tell he was thinking about how to respond. "She's on a whirlwind book tour right now. I'm sure Meriah will drop by when she's finished."

"I never heard the details of the birth. How did it go?" I asked, not that I actually cared, but I was tired of Franklin going after Shaneika.

Matt's face lit up. "At first Meriah was not going to let me take part, but when the contractions started, she asked for me. I followed her right into the birthing room and shared in the entire birth process. It was one of the most wonderful experiences anyone could have. I got to see my baby born." Matt's eyes teared up. "I'll be forever thankful that she allowed me to witness my daughter's birth."

Franklin jeered, "And once Meriah squeezed it out, she kicked the baby to the curb."

"That's not correct, Franklin," snapped Matt, his blue eyes flashing.

"I know what I saw."

Matt looked around the table. "Meriah had a difficult birthing. She was in labor for a very long time. It took a toll. Then she succumbed to postpartum depression, so naturally I took over the baby's care."

"Meriah went back to writing and parties as soon as she could drag herself out of bed."

"Franklin, that's unfair. Meriah loves the baby. She calls every night. She just doesn't have the baby gene like you do."

Franklin sniffed, "Whatever you say."

"She's a beautiful baby, Matt," offered Mrs. Dupuy. "I hope you're not shy about asking me to babysit."

Matt's face brightened, "Really? That would be wonderful. Even with Franklin and the nurse, she can be overwhelming at times. We all need a break now and then. I know she would be safe with you."

Mrs. Dupuy nodded as she gazed softly at Charles. "I know what you mean. If I hadn't had Charles' mother to help me, I would have gone out of my mind, especially since my first girl had the colic. She cried constantly for six weeks. My mother-in-law was a saint for helping me. "Newborns can be a handful. Matt, don't you be shy. If you need some time, give me a call. I love babies, and it won't bother me to watch over that sweet thing for a couple of hours."

I hoped nobody noticed that I wasn't volunteering to babysit. As a rule, I don't understand all the fuss about babies. I'd rather have a puppy.

I stood and raised my glass. "Here's to our friendship and the bonds that bind us as a people and a culture."

"Here. Here." said some. "Amen," hummed others as we all stood and clicked our glasses.

We were feeling pretty good about ourselves when Malcolm, one of the grandsons, entered the dining room. He came over and whispered in my ear. Nodding, I folded my napkin and said, "Excuse me. I have a telephone call." Following Malcolm into the hallway, I picked up the receiver, "Hello?"

"Josiah, is that you? This is Bunny Witt of the Philadelphia Witts. Do you remember talking to me in New York?"

I rolled my eyes. "Yes, Bunny. How on earth did you track me down?"

"I called the number June gave me, but no answer. I thought maybe you might be visiting her, so I gave her number a try. Clever, huh?"

"Yes, you'd make a great detective."

"You think so?"

"What can I do you for, Bunny?" I sat down suspecting this call was going to take awhile.

"Josiah, you won't believe it, but someone has been rifling through my things here in Lexington."

"How do you mean?"

"Just like before in New York. Nothing has been taken, but things are out of place. Even my personal papers are out of order."

"When did this take place?"

"It happened before I arrived. I'm sure of it."

"I think you should call the police. This seems to be getting out of hand. It may be nothing or you may be in danger. You won't know until you have more information."

"I don't know what to do. I am beside myself."

"Are you alone at the apartment?"

"Yes."

"Who knows you are in Lexington?"

"I don't know. Everyone. No one."

"What does that mean, Bunny?"

"The first thing I did after getting off the plane was check in with the exhibit director about my dresses. I wanted to make sure they had arrived in good condition."

Sighing, I said, "That means everyone knows you're in Lexington."

"I guess so. Was I wrong to do that? Anyway, when I got back to my apartment, I noticed straightaway that things were amiss."

"Is there any security at your apartment?"

"Some strong locks, that's all."

"They don't seem to be strong enough. Do you have any relatives you can stay with?" I could tell she was hinting at staying with me, but I had enough problems of my own. Besides, it sounded like Bunny had a stalker problem. Stalker issues usually end up with someone being injured or dead. I had learned this lesson the hard way, and I didn't want to take on another stalker having so recently rid myself of my own.

"Jo, tell Bunny she can stay with me while she's in Lexington."

"June, are you listening on the extension?" I asked.

"Of course I am. That's why I refuse to get a cell phone. How can I snoop on those things? Landlines are so useful for listening in unobtrusively."

"June, is that you?" asked Bunny.

"Yes, dear. I already said so. If you wish, you can stay with me until Josiah captures your stalker."

"Hold on there. I'm not capturing anyone. One stalker in a lifetime is enough for me, thank you. Bunny needs to call the police or hire a detective."

"You mean you won't help me?" asked Bunny in a trembling voice.

"I can't help you, Bunny. I'm in no shape mentally or physically to help anyone. I'm sorry."

"Can you at least fetch her?" inquired June.

Sensing a pair beady eyes staring at the back of my neck, I looked up, and there was June, glaring at me from the second floor balcony, looking rather put out.

Feeling rather guilty, since June stood by me through thick and thin with my travails with Fred O'nan, I caved in. "I'm coming to get you, Bunny. What's your address?"

"Oh, thank you. Thank you. I'll be ready in a jiffy."

I wrote down the address. "Make that half an hour. I'll honk the horn." Hanging up the receiver, I yelled to June. "Can I borrow Liam?"

"He's gone to Ireland for a visit with his family. He won't be back for several weeks," June yelled back.

"Jumping Jehosaphat," I muttered to myself.

"I'll go with you."

I looked up.

Matt was standing beside me. "You shouldn't go alone."

"Are you sure?"

"I've got to get away from Nurse Ratched for a few hours."

"What about the baby?"

"Franklin can watch her. He's practically lactating anyway. She'll be in good hands." He gave me a pleading look. "Please! I want to do something normal without a bunch of women hovering over me."

"Does that include me?" accused Franklin, lounging in the doorway.

"YES!" shot back Matt. "I just want an hour or two pretending that I'm like I used to be–whole."

"I understand," pouted Franklin. "I'll keep the baby while you gallivant around town with Josiah."

"Thanks, buddy."

Franklin smirked. "Josiah, see how low I've sunk on the totem pole. I was a boyfriend, then a close confidant, then a casual friend, and now I'm the babysitter. If it gets any worse, I'll be the dog walker."

"Franklin, I wouldn't trust my baby girl with just anyone. Only special people."

"Ooh, listen to that. Special people. Special people who get to change poopy diapers and clean up milk spit-up. I'm so thrilled."

Matt started to retort, but Franklin cut him off by waving his hand in a flimsy manner. "Go on. I'll watch the princess. Bring me back some chocolate ice cream, the expensive kind."

Matt gave Franklin a loving smile. "You're the best."

If Franklin noticed the intimacy of Matt's expression, he kept it to himself. "I keep telling you that. Two hours is all you get, *buddy*."

"Received and noted," replied Matt. He turned to me, "Shall we go?"

"Take the Bentley. I'll have one of the boys drive you," yelled June, meaning one Charles' grandsons. "Malcolm's been begging me to let him drive the Bentley. This is his lucky day."

Malcolm burst through the door that led to the kitchen. "You gonna let me drive the Bentley?" Obviously, he had picked up June's bad habit of eavesdropping.

"Yes, and bring it back in good condition. It's going to be yours one day. Treat her like the lady she is."

Malcolm grinned, "Yes, ma'am!"

"Skedaddle, now," urged Franklin. "I expect you back within two hours."

47

One of the farmhands had carved a gentleman's cane out of a tobacco stick for Matt, so he gathered his and I gathered my silver wolf's-head cane while following Malcolm, teetering on our walking sticks out to the garage.

Matt rode shotgun while I got into the back. Within a half hour we were sitting in front of Bunny's apartment in Hanover Court, a very old section of Lexington.

We sent Malcolm in to fetch Miss Bunny. A few minutes later, he came back, but without Bunny Witt of the Philadelphia Witts.

"Where is she?" Matt asked.

Malcolm looked worried. "No one answered the door. I knocked real loud. A neighbor poked her head out and said she hadn't heard Miss Bunny go out today."

"That doesn't sound good," I remarked.

"We'd better go up again. Rennie, you stay here," cautioned Matt.

"Sounds fine to me," I replied. I didn't really want to see if something gruesome had happened to Bunny.

Matt followed Malcolm into the yellow brick pre-WWII building, which had into six stunning apartments. It would take Matt a little time to climb the stairs to the third floor where Bunny lived.

I got out of the Bentley and leaned against the car while perusing the neighborhood for anything out of kilter. Several walkers stopped and admired the car, asking questions about it. I could tell they were just curious about the beautiful machine and posed no threat to me, but that didn't keep me from having my hand in my coat pocket wrapped tightly around my Taser.

Who's paranoid? Not me! I thought I told you that.

When Matt and Malcolm didn't return or yell out the window, I became concerned. Pulling out my cell phone, I began to dial Matt's number when I heard the scream of an ambulance getting louder and louder. It raced into Hanover Court and screeched to a halt in front of the Bentley.

An upstairs window opened and Malcolm stuck his head out. "Up here. Hurry!"

Since Malcolm had left the keys in the Bentley, I quickly moved it so the ambulance could get closer to the apartment building. After parking down the street, I got out and waited while people emerged from their beautiful nineteenth-century homes and clogged the street gawking.

Soon a police car arrived, and who should stumble out? Detective Goetz!

Hadn't he retired yet?

I hadn't spoken to Goetz for a long time, and I didn't want to speak to him now. I ducked behind a massive oak tree, peeking around occasionally.

What the hell was going on? What had happened? Where was Bunny? Did Matt have a relapse?

Whatever was happening, it seemed that Malcolm was taking charge. I saw him talking to Goetz as the grizzled cop took notes.

I smiled. There was that ratty notebook and that nubby pencil Goetz always carried.

Maybe I should say hello.

No. That wouldn't be prudent.

What would I say?

Thank you for killing O'nan and saving my life, but I'm sorry–I don't want to go to bed with you.

I had told Goetz earlier that year that I didn't want to see him anymore.

After I said it, he didn't say anything. He just gave me a strange look and walked away. I hadn't seen him since.

I was grateful to Goetz, but I wish he hadn't told me he had killed O'nan. I was worried that he would regret telling me and do something about it, afraid that I might squeal. So now I had someone else to worry about.

Or maybe I was too guilty over Matt getting shot by O'nan to seek my own happiness. If Goetz had taken aim sooner, Matt would never have been hurt. Maybe I blamed Goetz for that.

I feel bad about Matt's injuries. Real bad.

And truth be told, I'm slowly dying. There, I said it. You can't live without kidneys. But I was not going to snooze in my coffin yet. I needed to help Matt get back to his old life. I wasn't ready to throw in the towel just yet and felt I still had a lot of living left to do. I wasn't going to give up so easily. What's that Dylan Thomas poem about rage, rage against the dying of the light? That's me.

I hung around the fringes of a little knot of spectators so I could get closer to the action. At long last, two paramedics carried out a gurney with Bunny on it mewing like a newborn kitten. Next followed Matt offering encouragement.

Looking around, Matt spied me and beckoned.

Goetz followed Matt's look until he found me too.

I had to acknowledge Goetz now.

Wriggling my way through the crowd, I finally came face-to-face with Matt, who was in deep conversation with Goetz.

I heard Goetz tell him, "Matt, that case is still open. We don't know who shot O'nan. Why?"

Matt replied, "Because I want to send that son-of-a-gun a case of Pappy Van Winkle bourbon. He saved both Josiah and me that day at Cumberland Falls."

"He wasn't fast enough to save you from a bullet."

"I'm positive that once O'nan drowned Josiah, he would have come back on the rocks and finished me off with a shot between the eyes."

"I think he would have had to. You were a witness."

Seeing me for the first time in months, Goetz asked, "Josiah, who do you think killed O'nan?"

I stared right at him when I said, "I don't know, and I don't care. I'm just thankful that someone put that rabid dog down."

Goetz grunted.

"Goetz, it was great to see you. I've given all the information I can about Bunny Witt. Can I go back up to her apartment?" asked Matt.

Goetz glumly shook his head. "Naw. It's a crime scene. I'll have one of my tech boys go over it since Mrs. Witt was attacked. Then I want a look-see myself. Let me know if you think of anything else," he replied, walking away without even casting an eye in my direction.

He acted as though I didn't exist.

I don't know why, but it bothered me.

7

"This is so wonderful of you to take me in, June. Thank goodness the doctors said nothing was wrong with me," gushed Bunny, as she sank into a plush leather couch in Lady Elsmere's library. Light from the fireplace flickered on the glossy, oiled walnut panels that held thousands of books. Many were expensive first editions and priceless books printed in Europe soon after the invention of the Gutenberg Press.

I never thought a hot fire in a library was proper conservation of rare books, but it wasn't my money.

Sitting in a leather chair opposite June and Bunny, I gazed through the French doors to watch the sun setting across the well-manicured fields that made up June's estate. Farmhands were leading the mares into the barns for the night, their foals following contentedly beside them.

The mention of my name brought my attention back to Bunny's prattle.

"Jo, take your tea," commanded June.

A tea cup was thrust into my hands. I followed the arm holding the tea cup and caught a worried look from Charles.

"Oh, sorry, Charles. Thank you," I replied as I took the tea cup.

Knowing which tea cakes and biscuits I liked, Charles filled a plate and set it on the stand next to me.

I spied the laden plate with glee. Yummy!

June asked, "Jo, are you listening?"

I could tell she was put out. "My apologies again. I was just watching the horses being brought in for the night. It's so lovely this time of day. I think the old-timers call it the gloaming."

June glanced out the French doors. "Yes, it's lovely. Bunny, you're going to have to start over. Pay attention, Josiah."

"Yes, ma'am," I said, stuffing a bite-size chocolate-raspberry tea cake in my mouth. "Go ahead, Bunny. I'm all ears."

Bunny gave me a cautious glance, as if she didn't really believe me, but started droning her story over again.

Aw, geez.

"Well, I arrived home yesterday, and everything seemed fine. This morning I went to get groceries, and when I got back, I noticed some of my things had been disturbed."

"Like what?" I mumbled with my mouth full.

"I noticed that the pillows on my couch had been moved. They were out of order."

"Okay. Then what?" I asked.

"I must have cried out. Then I heard someone behind me, and as I was turning, I got hit on the head. I don't remember anything until I came to in the apartment with two men standing over me calling for an ambulance."

"You left some things out, Bunny," I said.

"Did I?"

"You made at least two telephone calls before you were hit. You made one to my house, and then to Lady Elsmere's house where we talked."

Bunny looked fearful. "I don't remember. I truly don't."

June interceded, "Josiah, it's common for people not to remember details after an accident."

"I know that, but it's important that Bunny try to remember as much as possible. Let's go over everything again."

"If you think it would help."

"Well, Bunny, it's not me that's getting conked on the head. If you'd rather not, that's fine by me. I've got other things to do."

Bunny grabbed my arm, which was holding a cup, causing me to spilled a spot of tea on the carpet.

June's mouth tightened, but hey, it wasn't my fault.

"Let's start when I last saw you in New York."

"All right."

"Did you tell anyone where you were going?"

"No."

"Did you tell your girlfriend?"

"No."

"Not even your assistant?"

"I did exactly as you told me, Josiah."

"You got on the plane."

"Yes."

"Did you see anyone on the plane that you knew or that you noticed?"

Bunny thought for a moment. "No. I didn't see anyone who caused alarm."

"Which flight did you take?"

"The direct night flight from New York."

"The 8:15?"

"Yes."

"How did you get to your apartment?"

"I took a cab."

"Did you notice anyone following you?"

"No, but I wasn't looking, either."

"What happened when you got to your apartment?"

"It was a late flight. I went straight to bed."

"Did you notice anything out of whack?"

"Nothing. Things were how I had left them."

"Then what happened?"

"The next morning I went to the store, and when I got back, I noticed the pillows on the couch were out of order. I notice things like that."

"You called me at home, and then you called here."

"Yes, that's right."

"Did you call anyone else?"

"No."

"How did you make the call?"

"On my new cell phone. The new one you told me to get."

"Would you get your phone for me, please?"

"You want to look at my phone?"

"Yes, Bunny, I do. Right now."

"Very well. It's in my room." Bunny reluctantly got up to fetch her phone.

Once she left the library, I peeked into the hall to make sure she was out of earshot. "She's lying," I told June. "Bunny keeps changing the details of her story."

"What makes you say that, Josiah?"

"She said on her phone call to me here that she went to check on her dresses first, and met with the director. That means she came in on an earlier flight and not the direct flight from New York, which leaves at 9:40 and not the 8:15. That flight gets in at midnight. Why would Bunny lie about her flight time?"

Saying nothing, June took a sip of tea. I could tell she was thinking over what I said.

"Since you were eavesdropping, I'm sure you heard her say that. Bunny is not the only one fibbing. Liam is not in Ireland seeing his family. What happened? Did you two have a fight and you kicked him out?"

Putting down her cup, June said, "My tea needs a little shot of bourbon. Join me?"

"Why the hell not?" I rose to get the bourbon decanter that was sitting in a book cubby. (Such decanters were strategically located throughout the mansion.) I poured a little into June's cup.

"Oh, honey," she purred, "just dump the damn bottle in the pot."

"Okey dokey," I replied, more than happy to oblige and defy my doctor once again.

We sat happily sipping our "tea" waiting for Bunny to come down with her phone. She took a very long time. By the time she entered the library again, I can't say I was soused, but I sure was in Happy Land.

"Here it is," she said, handing me the phone.

"How many numbers and messages did you erase? I know what you were doing. It doesn't take that long to tinkle and gather your phone."

"What?" she blurted, startled.

"Write down all the numbers you erased."

Bunny whined, "June!"

June shrugged her shoulders. "There's no use lying to Josiah, my dear. She's like a hound. The truth will out. It's too bad that nosy nose of hers never worked with her husband, Brannon."

"Don't bring him up," I cautioned. "I'm doing you both a favor, so don't tick me off." I rose from my chair.

June held up her cup and saluted me. "Where are you going?"

"You don't need to know. I'll be in touch."

"You're taking my phone?" cried Bunny.

"Just use the landline here," I suggested before I swept out of the room. I headed down the massive hallway and into the kitchen, where I found Charles feeding a half-starved, mangy mutt.

Charles looked up. "Found him on the farm. Looks like he was dumped."

"Maybe he has a chip."

"Taking him to the vet tomorrow to see. Right now, he needs a bath and warm place to bed down." Charles pointed to some dark spots on the dog's reddish fur. "Looks like bite marks to me."

I leaned over to see. "Yep. Maybe he was used in dog fighting."

Charles' face clenched into a fury. He hated to see animals mistreated. "I'll know better when I take him to the vet."

Bess walked in with a basket of freshly-picked spring greens. "Daddy, get that nasty dog out of my clean kitchen. We have lots of barns where you can take him. I don't know why you'd bring that filthy animal here."

Charles hurriedly picked up the animal and scurried out of the kitchen with me following. I got into my golf cart. "Charles, hop in. I'll take you to a safe haven."

"Take me to Barn Three. It's got hot water. I can give him a nice, soothing bath there."

I looked down at the dog clinging to Charles as though he were a life jacket. "Charles, are you going to continue raising racehorses after June passes?"

"I don't know, Josiah. I'd kind of like to take some of the pastures and at least one of the barns to make a home for distressed animals. That's my real passion, but I love the racing game too. I guess I haven't made up my mind yet. Just mulling it over."

I looked at the dog's pleading eyes staring up at Charles. "I'm sure you'll make the right decision, whatever you decide, Charles."

I stopped in front of Barn Three. "You know, Charles, if you want to bring rescue animals here now, June wouldn't mind. She wants you to start making your own decisions on what to do with the property."

"She's very frail. I don't want to do anything that might upset her."

"I don't think a couple of rescue goats and llamas grazing next to her racehorses is going to throw June into a tizzy."

Charles got out with the trembling dog. "I'll study on it."

"Where's Liam, Charles?"

"Can't say. That information needs to come from Her Ladyship."

"But you know?"

"Can't say that either."

"What happens in the Big House stays in the Big House?"

"It doesn't have anything to do with you."

"That's a first, then. See you later," and off I went to get my car.

The dog yipped a feeble good-bye.

How did I know that mangy mutt would play a pivotal role in solving the case?

8

Winston Churchill once said that tact was the ability to tell someone to go to hell in such a way that they look forward to the trip. However, my friends never bothered to sugarcoat the truth. They just blurted it out. At least my buddy Ray tried to be tactful.

I went to the city's old marble and limestone library where some of Bunny's dresses were being exhibited. Knocking on an oversized door, I let myself into the Executive Director's office without waiting for a reply.

Ray looked up. Surprised, he bounded up from his chair and heartily shook my hand. I'm not a hugger and thrust my hand out whenever I see someone attempt to latch their lumpy, sweaty body onto mine, or try to kiss my cheek with teeth full of debris from their last meal. A handshake will do nicely, thank you. That way I can rush to the bathroom and wash my hands.

Not that the current director was lumpy or sweaty or never brushed his teeth. Actually, he was quite a long, cool drink, as we say in the South. Know what I mean? Tall, dark, and handsome. A triple threat to the hormonal glands.

"What brings you here, Josiah Reynolds?" asked Ray.

"I want to take a look at Bunny Witt's dresses."

Ray raised an eyebrow. "Well, the exhibit's not ready for viewing. It's still being staged."

"I know that. I'm asking as a personal favor."

"I see."

"First, I would like to know how this old library got rooked into hosting this exhibit. This building is supposed to be about reading. It's not an art gallery."

"We were approached, as were many others. We like to accommodate important civic activities . . ."

I interrupted, "The Mayor's office leaned on you?"

"I didn't say that."

"Then who in the city convinced all the galleries in town to put on a show about couture? Who has that kind of pull?"

"A private citizen on behalf of an anonymous donor who wanted to put on this show, and would give us a substantial donation if we participated. We are going to use the money to expand our tutoring program for young people."

"Hmm. Have you received your donation yet?"

"The terms were that we would be presented a check on the gala opening night of the exhibit at Hilltop Manor."

"That's all they asked?"

"Yes. They just wanted this one exhibit."

"You didn't think that was strange?"

Ray grinned. "I get crazy requests all the time. As long as it's legal, in good taste, and somehow serves the community, we'll do it. Remember, we always exhibit local artists year round, so it wasn't a stretch to have a show about vintage couture."

"Who is backing this exhibit?"

"Can't tell you. Part of the request was that the donor remain anonymous."

"You don't think that's odd?"

"No. We have quite a few wealthy donors who wish to remain anonymous. They don't want people hounding them for money."

Ray certainly was keeping his cards close to his chest. If one door closes, go through another. "Did this anonymous donor request that Bunny Witt's clothes be exhibited?"

"No. Why are you so interested, Josiah? Is there something I should know?"

"But you have some of her outfits here?" I asked, ignoring his questions.

Ray's eyes narrowed. "Yes. I told you so. What's going on?"

"Can I count on your discretion?"

"You have to ask?"

"Bunny thinks someone is stalking her. Yesterday, she was attacked in her apartment."

Ray looked very concerned. "That's terrible."

"I'm beginning to think it might have something to do with this couture exhibit. She didn't notice things going awry until after she was asked to participate."

"What's your interest?"

"I was asked to check into it by Bunny."

Ray caught himself before he burst out laughing. "Josiah, I don't mean to be hurtful, but you look rather . . . um, tired. Don't you think the police would be more useful?"

I didn't take offense. The truth is the truth. "Ray, no truer words were ever spoken. I tried to tell Bunny Witt that, but she won't leave me alone."

Ray leaned over and patted my arm. "Take some advice from an old friend. Hire a PI for her and you go see a doctor. You don't look well."

Jumping Jehosaphat!!! How bad did I look?

9

I found nothing unusual with the couture exhibit at the old library. I spent several hours feeling hemlines, pockets, lapels, and linings to see if something was hidden. All I found was lint and one gum wrapper.

Disheartened, I left by the back staircase. I didn't want to run into Agnes Bledsoe, whose office was right across the street.

Agnes Bledsoe was the first wife of Richard Pidgeon, the man who was murdered in my bee yard. She didn't like me, and the feeling was mutual.

But whom did I run into?

You guessed it. Agnes Bledsoe.

"Agnes, hasn't the cancer gotten you yet?"

"Just like a hair on a biscuit–charming as ever, Josiah." She took a hard look at me. "You look like ten miles of bad highway. Who knows? I might be peeing on your grave."

I continued down the steps, saying, "That would be just my luck these days. What are you doing here, anyway?"

"I was headed to Gratz Park to eat my lunch and listen to the birds sing–that therapeutic crap I'm supposed to do."

"I know what you mean." I mimicked a doctor. *"I know your body's function is only thirty percent of what it used to be, but if you relax, you will feel much healthier."*

Agnes grinned. "Exactly. I know this might sound strange coming from me, but I've got a huge roast beef sandwich. Why don't you share it with me, and we can insult each other while we eat? If I could get your goat during lunch, I would feel so much better about my day."

Sometimes spending time with an enemy who just lets the manure fly is much more fun than being with a supposedly sincere friend who lies to your face. If you're like me, at least.

I accepted happily, but I picked out half the sandwich and handed it to Agnes to eat first, just in case she had sprinkled some rat poison on it.

I'm not being paranoid in this case–just prudent. We are talking about Agnes Bledsoe–remember?

We sat on a bench in the park and nibbled on the sandwich. I didn't actually think she would put rat poison on the sandwich, but I did think my running into her had been staged.

We didn't speak for a while, enjoying the beautiful park and the historic homes surrounding it. Finally, I said, "So, Agnes, what's up?"

"That's what I want to know."

"About what, exactly?"

"I'm hearing things through the grapevine."

"Such as?"

"First, I heard your boyfriend, Matt Garth, is back in town."

"He is in town, but he's not my boyfriend. He's gay," I shot back, sounding a little more defensive than I had intended.

"Oh, really? Then why was he going to marry Meriah Caldwell after he dumped you?"

"He backed out at the last moment because he's gay."

"So he tried to hustle her."

"No, he loved her but . . . look, Agnes, it's complicated. The man got shot trying to help me. I'm not going to say anything negative about Matt. Let's move on."

"I knew talking about Matt Garth would rile you."

I abruptly rose from the park bench. "If that's all you've got, I'm leaving."

Agnes waved her sandwich around. "Ah, don't get your granny panties in a wad. I'm just warming up."

I reluctantly sat back down. "Got anything sweet in that lunch sack?" If I had to endure a conversation with Agnes, there'd better be more in it for me than half a roast beef sandwich.

She rustled through her bag and pulled out a large chocolate chip cookie. "Here. Munch on this," Agnes said as she handed the cookie to me. "I'm not much on sweets. I tell my housekeeper no sweets, but she keeps putting cakes, cookies, you name it, into my bag."

"Maybe she's hoping the sugar will induce a diabetic coma."

Agnes decided to cut to the chase. "I hear something weird is going on with Bunny Witt."

"You mean Bunny Witt of the Philadelphia Witts, not to be confused with the Boston Whitts?"

Agnes licked her lips like a coyote when it locks onto a jackrabbit. I swear she did! "Spill. I heard someone attacked Bunny in her apartment."

"I guess it's no secret that someone hit her over the head."

"Any permanent brain damage?"

I shrugged. "It's like when Dorothy Parker was told President Calvin Coolidge had died, she quipped, 'How can you tell?'"

"Bunny has always been a little soft in the head."

"You know her?"

"Her parents more than her. They were important clients of mine. I've worked for Bunny a couple of years. She hasn't had a good racehorse in the longest time. Just plugs."

"She thinks she has a stalker problem."

Agnes' brow furrowed. "She might, you know. Do you know about the jewels?"

"She's never mentioned any jewels."

"I guess a lot of people have forgotten. Lady Elsmere might remember."

"Get to the point, Agnes."

"Her great aunt, or someone like that, had an affair with a raja, who gave her a fortune in cut stones."

"You mean like a prince from India?"

"Yes. This was before India gained its independence from Great Britain. Probably around the '20s or '30s of the last century."

Intrigued, I leaned forward. This little chat was producing a payout above and beyond a chocolate chip cookie.

Agnes continued. "I got the story from Bunny's mother. The great aunt had the stones fashioned into jewelry, and then the aunt got a little screwy in her old age. She had the stones removed from their settings and hid them without telling anyone where. To this day, no one has ever found them, and they're worth a king's ransom."

"So you think someone has learned of this story and is trying to find the gemstones?"

"It's a possibility." Agnes watched children playing in the fountain. "I was very fond of Bunny's mother. She was one of my first clients, and stood by me when I got my divorce from Richard. I would hate to see her daughter hurt."

"Bunny needs to hire a detective or involve the police. If she's truly being stalked, she's over her head going it alone," I advised.

"I think you're right. I think I'll call her and tell her to go the police."

Agnes stood. "I've got to get back to the office. When you see Bunny at Lady Elsmere's, encourage her to call the police, too." Agnes smirked and strode off into the sunset, so to speak.

I guess my mouth dropped open.

How did Agnes know Bunny was at Lady Elsmere's house?

LUCY, YOU GOT SOME 'SPLAININ' TO DO!

10

"Now listen to me, Bunny. If you want to be an idiot on your own time, that's fine. But when you involve June, that's different. How did Agnes Bledsoe know you were staying at the Big House with June? She said she had heard things through the grapevine."

Bunny's hands fluttered around her neck. "I feel like you're attacking me."

"Quit stalling. If you don't tell me what I want to know, I'm gonna haul off and punch your fat, pompous face. Now, give!"

"June, are you going to let Josiah talk to me like that?"

June lit a cigarette. "I can't control Jo. She's barely housebroken." Smoke blew out of her nostrils. "But I think you are taking advantage of my hospitality if you are running your mouth off about staying here, especially if you think a stalker is after you. That's not very nice,

Bunny, considering the trouble we have had with a
rogue cop who had it in for my Jo. We're still reeling
from the consequences.

"If you refuse to take Josiah's advice, I'm afraid I'll
have to cut you loose. I'm sure you think this seems
heartless, but unless you've been on the barrel side of a
gun, you can never know what trauma Jo's family and
mine have been through with all the people hurt due to
one deranged man."

Atta girl, June! Sic her! Somehow Bunny taking a
verbal beating from June made me feel good.

Bunny's mouth opened to form a perfectly round
circle, but no sound came out. Obviously, no one had
ever said no to her, let alone boo.

"Agnes told me an aunt of yours had a ransom in
gems, and that they disappeared. Any truth to that?" I
inquired.

Bunny smirked. "That old tale. Apparently my great-
great aunt did have lots of expensive stuff. I have
pictures of her wearing fabulous jewelry. Whether or not
she had an affair with a raja in India and he gave her the
jewelry is anyone's guess."

"But you can confirm that a relative of yours did have
a considerable wealth in gems?" I asked.

"Why yes. The story has been handed down through
the women of my family."

"What happened to the loot?"

Bunny shrugged. "No one knows."

I continued the interrogation. "Who inherited from this aunt?"

"My grandmother and then my mother."

"What did your mother inherit? And be exact." My tone was sharper than it needed to be but I was irritated with this dumb nut.

Bunny sighed as though she was thoroughly put out with June and me, and was humoring us at a great cost to herself. "My mother inherited all my great aunt's furniture, most of her clothes, some money. That's all."

"What about papers, books, diaries, maps?"

Bunny gave me a blank look. "I don't know. I wasn't even born yet. I would have no idea."

"Where would your great-great aunt's things be stored?"

"Well, I guess here in Lexington."

I assumed Bunny meant her apartment. You know what they say about people who assume—an ass out of u(you) and me. I was to realize what a dummy I was later.

"Where was your mother living when your aunt died?"

"Lexington."

I thought out loud. "Were your aunt's things shipped here?"

"I think so. I know my grandmother took the story of the gems seriously and looked for them for a long time before she gave up. My mother looked somewhat, but gave up the chase fairly quickly."

"Now, we're getting somewhere. Any relatives contest the will?"

Frustrated with all the questioning, Bunny shot back, "I would have no idea. That was before my time, as I stated."

'Did your mother sell things off?"

"Oh, no. Now that I know for sure. My mother believed the gems existed."

"Yes, I know," I replied. "I think you mentioned that."

"Did I? I must be getting tired. Are we quite finished?" Bunny put down her tea cup.

"Do you have a copy of the will or a list of the inventory?"

"I don't see what that old story has to do with my stalker," protested Bunny.

"Alas, I cast my pearls before Bunny, but I can't string them together for her," I preached.

"What's she talking about?" asked Bunny, her lips trembling.

"Josiah is making a veiled reference to pigs," remarked June, raising an eyebrow.

"Are you calling me a pig?" accused Bunny, her face turning red.

"I'm saying you don't listen. The story about the gems could have something to do with your intruder or not, but it needs to be investigated as a possible cause. You're putting us all in a pickle."

"Please don't send me away, June. I guess I wasn't

taking this seriously. It was terrifying but exhilarating that something finally was happening that involved me. Nothing exciting ever happens to me."

I saw that June's face was softening. *NO! NO! Throw the silly woman out, June! She's nothing but trouble.*

"If you promise to do as we ask, then you may stay," announced June, pointing a finger at Bunny, "but the moment you slip up, out you go."

My chin dropped to my chest. *Oh, well.*

"Whom else did you see, Bunny?" June asked.

"I went to see Mr. McPherson at Hilltop Manor, to ensure my dresses were properly installed. Most of them are there."

"Who is Mr. McPherson?" I asked wearily.

"He's the promoter of the exhibit."

"Your problems started when this exhibit was first announced, and you didn't bother to tell me about this McPherson? You didn't see a possible connection?" I demanded incredulously. I hate stupid people.

"Why goodness no," Bunny spouted. "Mr. McPherson has impeccable manners. One can tell he is of good breeding and a gentleman."

"People of good breeding stab others in the back all the time," I remarked as I rose. "I'm not getting involved in this anymore. I have to think of myself." I looked at Bunny. "I'm going to get you a PI and you are going to pay him what he asks, but stick a fork in me—I'm done." I strode out of the room with as much dignity as possible, but I truly had had enough.

11

I stopped by Matt's house, knocking and then walking in without waiting for someone to come to the door.

The house was eerily quiet.

Matt was sitting on the couch reading the paper. The nurse was in the kitchen feeding the baby. I glanced down the hall. Franklin was tidying up the baby's room.

I plopped down beside Matt and picked up a slice of toast from the coffee table. "What's up?" I asked.

Franklin poked his head around the corner. "I'll tell you what's wrong. This shack is too small. We're practically sitting on top of each other."

"You can stay with me," I offered.

Matt winced. "That's awfully kind of you, Rennie, but Baby's a concern," he said, referring to my one-eyed English Mastiff.

I drew back. "My Baby wouldn't hurt your baby! How dare you insult my friend."

Matt put his hand on my arm. "Baby has never been around a human baby, let alone a crying, fussy baby. And he's too protective of you. He might see the baby as a threat. No," he said, shaking his head, "I don't want to take the risk."

Franklin came in and sat in a chair. "Plus, Baby slobbers too much. Our baby would be covered in slime all the time."

"I'll grant you that," I replied, still reeling from the insulting idea that my dog might hurt a child.

Franklin continued, "Beside there are all those cats that come in at night. The baby could get cat scratch fever."

I thought for a moment. "Call June and tell her you're coming to stay with her."

"I couldn't do that," scoffed Matt.

"Why not? All you have to do is flirt with her and she'll turn the house upside down for you. I insist. You call her."

"I'll do it," said Franklin, yanking out his cell phone. He hurriedly dialed and then handed the phone to Matt.

Matt reluctantly took the phone. "Hello? Lady Elsmere?"

Hearing June on the other end, I grabbed another piece of toast and headed home to my big, menacing, slobbery dog, Baby.

I was certain June would love having Matt and the baby, but I knew Bunny wouldn't.

It was a small thing, but still a payback. I just love being a stinker sometimes. I grinned all the way home.

12

I had received a call that my new bees were in, so Malcolm and I hopped in a truck "borrowed" from Lady Elsmere, and made fast tracks to Frankfort, where an entire truckload of bees had just arrived.

I let Malcolm drive, which might have been a mistake, but I just shut my eyes when he careened around those hairpin curves on the back roads. To my surprise, we arrived safely, as did about thirty other beekeepers waiting to pick up their packages of bees.

Maneuvering through throngs of vehicles and anxious beekeepers, Malcolm parked the truck in one of the few parking spots still available.

"Josiah, I can get the bees. You sit here."

I already had my door open and was easing myself down to the ground. "Not on your life. I want to check those packages before we accept them."

As usual with teenagers, Malcolm shot ahead to hang with other young men he knew and left me in the dust, which meant I had to tug a little wagon along to carry my new packages of bees.

I've never been the most graceful of creatures, even before my accident, but with my limp, I'm positively a fright. Of course I exaggerated my limp, since I didn't want to stand in line for an hour to get my bees. By making sure I caught the attention of many beekeepers, most of them men, I was quickly bumped up to the front of the line.

"Howdy, Jo. Get in front of me. You shouldn't be standing."

"Hello, Josiah. It's been awhile. Still selling at the Farmer's Market? You don't look so hot. Hey guys, let Josiah Reynolds up to the front of the line."

"Hey there, Josiah. Take my place. I see some people I need to talk to anyway."

I've also been known to exaggerate my limp in grocery store lines and for plane boardings.

Don't judge me. I mean it. Don't. If you're a woman, you've got to grab the wolf by the throat anyway you can.

In a few short minutes, I was at the front of the line looking at a mound of 200 buzzing packages, each weighing three pounds, and containing thousands of bees, including a Queen and her court.

After examining my bee packages and judging them to be healthy, I called for Malcolm, prying him away from the pack of young male beekeepers. Reluctantly, he bid them good-bye, doing that fist-bumping thing young men do these days, and hurried over.

With little effort, Malcolm secured the boxes in the back of the truck and laid a tarp down to protect my babies from the wind, but to also quiet the bees. Sunlight stimulates honeybees. We wanted them in the dark so they would remain calm for the trip home.

Within an hour, Malcolm and I pulled into my bee field, where he stopped in front of some empty hives.

I had lost fifteen hives due to the harsh winter before, and would now be able to repopulate ten empty hives with the new bees. I would split my older hives to make up the rest of the loss.

Even though honeybees are usually gentle when they are being transferred to a new hive, I was still cautious.

Malcolm and I donned veils and gloves, making sure the bottoms of our pant legs were taped. Nothing is more irritating that a stray bee finding her way into your pants and traveling up your leg to sting the tender part of your thigh. Yaweee! That hurts.

Malcolm lined up the rectangular boxes so I could lightly spray the bees with water. The water on their wings keeps the bees from flying into the air when released. The boxes are made up of ninety percent screen fabric to which the bees cling—in case you're wondering.

Using his penknife, Malcolm carefully extracted the queen cage from the top of the package and handed it to me. I checked the Queen. This one was moving vigorously inside the cage, indicating she was healthy.

I slowly unplugged the cork from one entrance of the queen cage with a sharp tool and then inserted the cage between two frames in the hive. That entrance was filled with candy, which the bees would eat through to release their new Queen.

Once this was achieved, Malcolm turned the package upside down and shook 10,000 bees onto the frames and the queen cage. Some bees immediately covered the queen cage, attracted by the Queen's pheromones, while others fled deeper into the hive.

After watching the bees descend into the hive, I nodded to Malcolm, and he put the inner cover on. I placed some bee pollen patties and sugar water on top of the inner cover, which had a hole that the bees could use to travel to their emergency food. Then another top called the outer cover was added.

To seal the hive, I pulled grass to stuff in the main entrance, making sure the bees were blocked from leaving. For three days, the hive would remain closed, giving the bees time to accept their Queen and she could settle in.

On the third day, the hive would be opened and the queen cage checked. If all had gone well, the Queen would be free by the bees by eating through the candy plug. If not, I would release her from the cage. Then the front of the hive will be opened to let the honeybees do their honeybee thing.

We had installed five packages when I spied Matt walking through the fields toward us with his bee suit on.

Matt stumbled and fell.

I turned away in embarrassment, not knowing what to do, but Malcolm saved the day.

"Matt, quit clowning around. Get your butt over here and help."

Chuckling, Matt righted himself, apparently with his pride and body unhurt.

Grateful for the fact that Matt couldn't see my tear-filled eyes, I pulled the next box toward the end of the tailgate and waved to Matt. "She's all yours!"

"It's so good to be working with bees again. It's like working with one of God's miracles," Matt observed.

"I've never known you to be so philosophical, Matt," I said.

"Never had a baby before. Children make you see things differently."

"How well I know," I replied, handing him my hive tool before feeling something brush against my legs. I let out a cry and did a little hop. The last thing I wanted was a curious skunk visiting to see what all the hoopla was about.

"Who's that little rascal?" asked Matt, pointing to my side.

I looked down, relieved to see that it was the old, gnarly, stray dog Charles had rescued. "How you doing, boy? Got tired of staying in the barn?" I reached down and scratched his ears. "Charles found this old boy and has made him his new best friend."

"Really?" Matt leaned down and petted the dog's muzzle while examining him. "Looks kind of beat up."

Malcolm chimed in, "Pops thinks he was used as dog-fighting bait and then dumped. He's spent a small fortune on vet bills for this old mutt."

The dog retreated several feet away and lay down in the tall grass, watching us.

"Huh. He seems awfully friendly in that case. You'd think he'd be traumatized," muttered Matt as he pulled down his veil while I sprayed the bees. With clocklike precision, Matt had the last packages of bees tucked in their hives in record time. He kept glancing over to see if the dog remained.

It seemed to me the dog intently followed Matt's every motion.

Finally the job was finished. Malcolm put in the last of the food and closed the hives.

"Let me check on the Queens in three days," Matt requested.

Picking up the empty cages, Malcolm offered, "I'll help you, Matt. Just let me know."

"That's great. I'll be busy the next several days. Matt, are you sure you're up to it?" I asked.

"Yes, Rennie. Quit hovering. In fact, leave the bees to me. I'll even do the hive splits if Malcolm can help me. Working with them relaxes me. I think even the venom in their stings helps my joints."

"No problem, Matt. I like them too, even though they are ornery little cusses," replied Malcolm.

"That's such old time talkin' from a young guy like you," I teased.

Malcolm grinned. "Been reading that diary of Henry Clay's that Lady Elsmere gave to Pops last Christmas. Getting back to my roots. Think I'll take some history courses in college next fall."

"Oh, Malcolm, that would please your grandfather so much," I gushed, peeking at my watch. "Guys. I've got to run. I'm supposed to help Mrs. Todd. Talk to you later."

Malcolm reached into his pants pocket to retrieve his truck keys. "I'll run you back."

"Stay put. I'll be fine. The house is not too far, and I need the exercise. I've got my phone. If I need help, I'll buzz you." I hurried toward the Butterfly, my home on the palisades, with just one last backward glance at the bee yard. I had days better than others, when my legs felt strong. Today was a good day, and I wanted to take advantage.

Malcolm was busy inspecting the other hives, while Matt was lying in the grass next to the mutt. The dog placed a paw on Matt's shoulder. They both looked contented.

I uttered a small prayer of thanks.

13

As I approached the Butterfly, I was astonished to see an all-too-familiar car in the driveway–a fire engine red Avanti! What the hell did he want?

I pushed through the front doors where a flabbergasted Eunice Todd met me. "Where is he?" I asked brusquely as she helped me off with my gear.

"Having coffee in the great room," Eunice murmured. "He wouldn't take no for an answer."

"Coffee," I scoffed. "You mean coffee laced with my good bourbon!"

I rushed to the great room that overlooks the palisades on the Kentucky River.

Walter Neff was out by the pool gaping down the cliff.

I went out. "How are you, Walter?"

Walter Neff spun around. "I'm a milk bone in a dog-eat-dog world, Josiah. Miss me?"

"Every flea and tick season."

Walter laughed. "That's my girl. Fat and sassy, although I would say that you could stand to put on a few pounds. You look positively gaunt. What happened to the love handles you were packing? You know I like a little meat on my women. Somethin' to grab onto."

When I didn't respond, Walter gestured to the cliff. "So this is where it happened? The great fall." He whistled, mimicking something falling and then crashing. "Must have hurt like a son-of- . . ."

"How did you know the code to get through the front gate?"

"My client was kind enough to provide me with it."

Of course it had to be Bunny. Who else would be stupid enough to give out the code to my electronic gate, but how did she get it? "What brings you here, Walter?"

"Toots, you cut me to the quick. Okay. I see how it is. Can I sit down at least?"

"Don't bother. You won't be staying that long."

Walter recoiled as though he had been slapped. "Still holding a grudge? I guess I can understand that, but I forgave you for backstabbing me. I'm willing to let bygones be bygones. What about you, Toots?"

I heard the back door open and knew Eunice had let Baby out onto the back patio. Baby moseyed over and stood in front of me, leaning into my legs in a protective stance. He turned his massive head toward

Walter as a string of doggie slobber slowly sank to the ground.

Walter's eyes grew big. "Yikes. I forgot about that monster of a dog." He leaned forward, at which Baby issued a growl. "I see where O'nan shot him and also why. He's massive."

Baby growled again.

"WALTER!"

Walter jerked up, reaching into his pocket. He pulled out a tattered journal. "Your good friend, Bunny Witt, has hired me to investigate the break-ins to her homes as per your suggestion. She told me that you thought there might be a connection between her great aunt and the break-ins. She gave me the old lady's diary. I can't make heads or tails out of it. It's written in old lady scrawl." He tossed the book on the patio table. "You read it, Toots. You're good at stuff like that. I'll cut you in if there is a bonus."

I was at the point of curtly refusing and tossing Walter out on his ear when he shot one of his signature salacious grins and tipped his pork pie hat at me. "I'll see myself out," and with that he was gone.

14

I wore myself out rehearsing the nasty things I was going to say to Bunny when next I saw her, and went to bed–exhausted and mad. I was going to return that diary and give Bunny a piece of my mind. Yes, sir. No buts about it!

15

I felt something nudge the bed. Slowly opening my eyes, I focused on a long strand of drool. "Baby, what do you want?" I asked, pushing the Mastiff's massive head away from mine.

Feeling a hot blast of fetid breath on my face, I exclaimed, "Gosh, your breath stinks! What do you want?"

Baby bounced his head on the mattress again while barking loudly.

"Okay. Okay. I'm getting up. Someone must have to go potty." I got up and let Baby out through my bedroom door. Mist from the river was rising and beginning to creep across the patio.

Baby went over to the diary, which I had left on the patio table, and barked. He turned to see if I was watching. Seeing that he had my attention at last, Baby went to the grass area and did his business. For some ridiculous reason, Baby always wants me to watch. Why do dogs do that? And do all dogs do that?

"Oh dear, I left that book out in the damp." I hurried over and retrieved the diary. Sitting in a chair while Baby sniffed various places in the grass and plants here and there, I surveyed the scenery. Hearing coyotes howl across the river, Baby began howling too.

"That does it. I'm not sitting out in the cold while you serenade your buddies. I'm going in," I told Baby.

He reluctantly followed, plodding his massive paws on the floor. It sounded like sandpaper scraping stone.

I spread the diary open so the pages would dry from the damp and went back to bed.

I had no idea that this mundane action would result in a lucky break for unlocking the diary's secrets, or that it would turn out to be so unlucky for Bunny.

16

Eunice was catering the big whoop-de-doo for the couture exhibit, so I tagged along when she had a meeting. Eunice took the back roads at a leisurely pace. We gaped, gawked, and generally gossiped about other people's property along the way until we entered the long drive to Hilltop Manor on Old Frankfort Pike, where the main exhibit was being held as well as the main reception and gala.

Hilltop Manor was an antebellum mansion which had been turned into an art gallery.

"I hope this guy doesn't want to have young girls parading around in hoop skirts serving Mint Juleps."

"Oh, heaven forbid," I mocked.

Eunice shot a severe look in my direction, but I ducked.

We climbed the huge limestone steps to the portico, and it took both of us to push through the massive walnut front doors.

"Good lord," I complained. "Don't they have a handicapped entrance?"

"It makes you wonder who they were trying to keep out," came a voice from the shadows.

Startled, both Eunice and I peered through the darkness of the entrance hall. Eunice barked, "Who said that?"

A tall, middle-aged man emerged from the shadows. He was sporting a pencil-thin mustache and was entirely too good-looking for his own good. "I'm so sorry," conveyed the man in a silky tone while he extended his manicured hand. "I didn't mean to startle you. My name is Thaddeus McPherson. I'm afraid I'm the curator of this exhibit, and I was to meet a Eunice Todd to discuss the reception."

Eunice leaned forward and shook his hand. "I'm Mrs. Todd. This is my friend, Josiah Reynolds."

"Mrs. Reynolds. Delighted to meet you both," he said as he shook my hand. He had a nice firm grip, but not crushing like some men. It was pleasant to the touch.

"Mrs. Todd."

"I don't mean to be forward, but I detect an accent. Are you British?" asked Eunice.

"I haven't been to my homeland for decades, but you've found me out. Born and bred Londoner. I'm afraid if you had met me thirty years ago, my accent would have been more cockney than anything else. Through the years, I've worn the rough edges off some. But, dear lady, I might add I hear a Bermuda lilt in your cadence."

Eunice gave Mr. McPherson a winning smile. "I had the privilege of running one of the finest hotels in Bermuda for over twenty years before coming home. I guess some of the island's ways rubbed off on me."

"And what a charming lilt it is. I have had the pleasure of visiting Bermuda several times. It's breathtakingly beautiful. Those pink beaches." He gave us both that dazzling smile again.

I was tempted to shield my eyes from the white glare of his teeth. I also noticed dimples when he smiled, which gave him an impish look. I wondered how many women Mr. McPherson had charmed with those dimples.

Clapping his hands, Mr. McPherson said, "Ladies, if you follow me, we can discuss the venue in a private office. Mrs. Todd." He gestured toward the hallway.

"Call me Eunice, please," she gushed.

"Then you must call me Teddy."

"I'll wait here," I said in a near whisper. "I'm just a tag-a-long. Eunice is your gal."

"Oh, I see." Teddy said, fiddling with the flower boutonnière on his grey three-piece suit. "Please feel free to take in the exhibit while you wait."

"Thank you. I think two of my dresses are here."

"Which ones would that be?" inquired Teddy, looking at me with renewed interest.

"Two Roberto Capucci dresses."

Suddenly exuberant, Teddy pontificated, "Those are the only Roberto Capucci dresses we have in the exhibit.

The rest of the Lexingtonian ladies don't seem to share your aesthetic sense of couture. We have too many examples of shoulder-padded, sequined dresses by Bob Mackie," Mr. McPherson said with dripping sarcasm, "but Capucci's dresses are works of art. Don't you agree? Everything he does is fabulous."

"Yes, I quite agree."

Not to be outdone, Eunice added, "My daughter has over fifteen dresses in the exhibit. Most of them are Chanel."

"You must take in the exhibit as well, and tell me what you think. I hope you discover that the exhibit is as fine as any couture display in the world. In fact, I have several friends who are famous designers and are flying in just to see this exhibit." He turned to my friend. "So Eunice, you see why we must have the very best gala."

"Of course. I only do the very best," agreed Eunice.

"Please excuse us, Mrs. Reynolds, but I must whisk Eunice away to discuss the details." He smiled again. It was like a lighthouse splashing beams of bright light into the foyer.

Once again I was tempted to shield my eyes from the glare. "Take your time," I said. "I'll be fine."

Eunice nodded and fell into step with Mr. McPherson down a long dark hallway, no doubt illuminated by his teeth.

Curious to see how my dresses were displayed, I moseyed into the main exhibit hall. I was aghast. Wait, that's not the right word. I was astonished. The exhibit was a riot of color and textures of one-of-a-kind everyday wear, coats, and evening dresses. There were dresses from the 1700's to current day–every style imaginable. Not only was couture exhibited, but shoes, gloves, hats, handbags, luggage, and the most wonderful jewelry ever designed.

I had to admit the display was stunning. I didn't know where to look first. "There must be millions of dollars in this one room alone," I murmured to myself.

"Who knew dames spent so much money on their threads?"

I spun around. "Walter, what are you doing here?"

Walter Neff thumbed over his shoulder. "Here with the boss lady. She wanted to see her dresses."

I glanced over Walter's shoulder and spied Bunny clucking nervously around one of her dresses.

Walter fingered a silvery flapper dress covered in diamonds. "Do you think these rocks are real?"

"They're paste. Just rhinestones. If they were real diamonds, the dress would be too heavy to wear."

As soon as he knew the stones were fake, Walter lost interest and dropped the fabric like it was on fire.

"Still looking for that pot of gold at the end of the rainbow?"

Walter flashed a toothy smile. "The pot may be closer than you think."

"What do you mean?"

"Never you mind. Did you read that diary like I told ya?"

"No, I've been busy living my life. Besides, I don't do what men tell me to do. I stopped that foolishness a long time ago."

"I was counting on you."

"Your mistake."

"Come on, Toots. Help me out."

"I might if you tell me what you have found out so far."

"You were always a nosy broad."

"Does Bunny really have a stalker?"

"I think something is up, but I'm not sure what. It doesn't make sense–breaking into her apartments and taking nothing."

"What about the conk on her head?"

"Once Mrs. Witt was unconscious, the intruder could have done anything to her, but he just left. That proved to me this isn't about a sex freak getting his jollies sniffing her panties. And I've checked into her past. She's not into swinging or weirdo sex. Mrs. Witt might like multiple partners, but she likes them one at a time and in the missionary position."

While I was wondering how Walter came by that last piece of information, I asked, "That leaves revenge or money."

"Exactly what I was thinking. I'm still checking into her exes."

"Don't forget employees."

"I know how to do my job," blustered Walter.

"JOSIAH!" squealed Bunny. She rushed over and gave me a big hug. "So nice to see you." She put her arm around Walter's waist.

I gave a Walter a curious look.

"I've been meaning to call you, but I've had so many things on my plate, I haven't had the time."

"That's all right." I wanted to berate her for giving out the code to my farm gate, but seeing her with Walter made me curious, so I kept quiet.

She snuggled even closer to Walter.

I shot Walter another look that he returned with a sheepish grin. "I'm glad that you finally took my advice and hired a PI."

"I am too. I hired this delicious hunk of man and feel so much safer now. He's so strong and protective."

Walter? A delicious hunk of man? YIKES!

"And I wanted to tell you I've moved out of June's house and moved into mine. I do appreciate June letting me stay with her, but honestly, I just couldn't stand the noise with that baby crying and the baby's father always so morose."

"Matt is recovering from a serious gunshot wound, you know."

"Well, I'm very sorry about that, but I don't see why I should have to suffer as well. After all, someone hit me on the head, and I'm not going around acting all depressed and put out. I don't think that man said five words to me while I was there."

If Bunny didn't notice the fury growing on my face, Walter certainly did. "Mrs. Witt, I think we need to go."

"Now don't rush me. I haven't finished talking to Josiah."

"So you moved back to your apartment?" I asked, choking down the anger.

"Certainly not. It's too small for Walter and me. I've opened the house."

"House?"

"Yes, Mommy's house on Bryan Station Road. It's big enough for Walter and me."

"You have both a house and an apartment in Lexington?" I asked incredulously.

"Oh, didn't you know? I like to be downtown so I usually stay in my apartment, but with all that's going on, I thought I'd better open Mommy's house."

"You didn't think you should have told me that you have a country home?"

Bunny's eyes widened. "I thought everyone knew I own Ravensnest Farm.

"Ravensnest?" I was starting to sound like a parrot. "You own that big mansion and that horse farm? I thought that was owned by the Breckenridge family."

"Yes, that's my mother's maiden name. It's the family name on my mother's side. She is of the Clay-Breckenridge stock. My father was a distant descendant of Commodore Vanderbilt. My legal name is Madeline Vanderbilt Breckenridge Witt, not to mention my various married names."

Abigail Keam

I shook my head. I was getting more stupid with each passing year. Of course she was a Breckenridge. Why hadn't I made the connection?

"I see. And Walter is staying with you?"

Bunny smiled coquettishly at Walter, who returned her smile, albeit weakly. "He's also acting as my bodyguard."

"I'm just curious. Why did you leave June's Big House again?"

Bunny rambled, "When I told June I couldn't stand all the noise in the house with that baby and then some horrible-looking dog growling at me every time I went to my room, I said 'June, can't you put them up someplace else on the farm.' She suggested I open Ravensnest, saying that staying with her was cramping my style, and then recommended Walter, like you did, saying I needed a bodyguard. I thought that was a splendid idea, and she did too. So here we are. Walter follows me around like my own shadow. I feel very safe in his protection." She giggled. "I'm repeating myself now."

"Walter, I've got to hand it to you. You certainly found your pot of gold at the end of the rainbow."

"Gold? Gold? What's she talking about, Walter?"

"Nothing, Mrs. Witt. I'll explain later." He pulled Bunny close. "When we're alone."

Bunny giggled while Walter winked at me. Locked arm-in-arm, they strode past me, both of them beaming like teenagers off to the prom.

Jumping Jehosaphat! Don't that beat all!

101

17

"I warned you not to let her stay at the Big House," I sniped, berating June.

"I know—I know, but her mother was such a gracious person. Oh my, her mother would roll over in her grave if she knew what a silly, vapid person Bunny is," June replied, lighting a cigarette.

"I think she might have had an idea before she croaked." I said, waving away the smoke. "I love that she gave you an ultimatum."

"I did see her predicament. The baby does cry like all babies, and that scruffy dog didn't like her. No matter how many times we put him out, that dog would find his way back into the house, so I finally told Bess and Amelia to let him stay."

"I'm sure they liked that."

"They don't like animals in the house, but what can I do? He doesn't cause any problems. He just follows Matt around and sleeps by the baby's crib."

"The dog has adopted them," I observed.

"Apparently. I told Amelia and Bess that as long as the dog doesn't make any messes or chew the furniture, he could stay–and that goes for Matt as well." She snorted with laughter.

"Why didn't you tell me Bunny owned Ravensnest?"

June waved her cigarette around, oblivious of the ashes fluttering down to the Persian carpet. "How am I supposed to know what is stored in your noodle and what is not? You didn't ask, so therefore I assumed you knew all about our Miss Bunny."

"How would I?"

"Gossip, dear girl, gossip. The thing that makes the world go round."

"I thought it was love that made the world go round. Speaking of love, when is Liam supposed to come back?"

June drew heavily on her cigarette before shrugging.

"Was Liam a bad boy while I was away in New York?"

Blowing smoke out through her nose, Lady Elsmere, surrounded in a shroud of grey, murmured, "Liam was a very bad boy. Very bad, indeed."

18

From the bench where I was waiting, I heard a door buzz open. I watched silently as Liam Doyle went to the open window and collected his belongings, signed for them, and then, with a hangdog expression, turned to me.

"Thank you, Mrs. Reynolds. I've been in that jail cell longer than I cared."

"Then I suggest that you not steal jewelry from guests of Lady Elsmere's. I assume she declined to pay your bail in order to teach you a lesson."

"Her Ladyship didn't send you?" asked Liam, his face crestfallen.

"No. Lady Elsmere said you had gone to Ireland to see your folks."

"Sure and begorra, she's really mad then, and meant to leave me in this hellhole to rot."

I looked around at the clean detention center. "I

would hardly call this jail a hellhole."

"What am I going to do now?"

"Tell me what happened."

"Lady Elsmere had friends over for a snort fest."

I broke in. "A snort fest?"

"That's what I call it. Ladies are invited for tea, but they always get stinking drunk, because they spike the tea with bourbon."

I tried hiding my smile, but wasn't doing a good job of it. "Go on," I encouraged.

"One of the ladies brought a necklace her husband had given her recently to show to the other ladies. I was helping Charles serve tea when she pulled the necklace out of her purse. She was raving about how much it cost. You know, blah, blah, blah. As she was showing it around, I got a good look at it. It wasn't what she said."

"Why was that?"

"She claimed it was a Harry Winston diamond and ruby necklace."

"And?"

"It was no such thing. I can tell glass a mile away. It was a fake, and not even a good one at that."

"Then what happened?"

"The guest put the necklace back in her purse."

"She just had the necklace loose in her purse? No box?"

"Just like that. So the ladies go up to Lady Elsmere's bedroom to look at Her Ladyship's jewelry collection, and I saw my opportunity."

"To steal."

"No, no. I wanted a better look at that necklace."

"So you went into the woman's purse and took out the necklace."

Liam nodded shamefacedly. "That's when Charles walked in and caught me red-handed inspecting the goods. I tried to explain, but he caused such a ruckus that the police were called, and here I stayed until you rescued me."

"That surprises me. I would think that Charles would have had you put the necklace back and then tell Lady Elsmere after the guests had left, so as not to embarrass anyone."

"That man never liked me, and saw his chance to get rid of me."

I frowned. "That doesn't sound like the Charles I know. For now, you will stay with me. I may need your expertise in the future." I pointed my finger at him and looked him squarely in the eye. "No funny business, Liam, or you go right back in the slammer."

"No, Madam. As God as my witness you can trust me."

I didn't reply. Liam was one of the last people I would ever trust, but he would have to do for now.

19

"Liam said he just wanted to examine the necklace. He said it appeared to be a fake and wanted a closer look."

"I don't care," barked Charles. "He was caught going through a guest's purse. Unthinkable." Charles shuddered.

"Charles, I'm surprised. I thought such a matter would have been handled in a more discreet manner, instead of hauling Liam off to jail and embarrassing Lady Elsmere."

June walked into the kitchen with Amelia. "I heard you badgering Charles, so I've come to his rescue."

"Charles, was I badgering you?" When he didn't respond, I gave him a raspberry. Childish, I know, but don't judge me.

June confessed, "Charles didn't call the police. I did. I warned Liam that he was not to ply his trade in my home. He broke the rules."

"Are you done with him?" I asked.

"Oh, goodness no. I just wanted to make Liam suffer a little bit before I took him back. Teach him a lesson."

"So you bailed him out?" asked Amelia.

"This morning," I replied.

"I wish you hadn't thrown your money away on that scoundrel," Amelia admonished.

Matt strode into the kitchen. "Hello. Is this a private conversation?"

June quipped, "We're simply berating Josiah for sticking her nose where it doesn't belong."

I made a face.

Matt smiled. "I couldn't help but overhear. I apologize, but voices carry in this house, so I called the DA, who is a buddy of mine. All charges against Liam have been dropped."

"How did that happen?" asked Charles, astonished.

"It appears that the lady in question had the necklace appraised, and it was, indeed, paste. She doesn't want everyone to know that her husband is a cheapskate, so she asked the DA to drop the charges, saying she would not testify. The matter has been handled quietly."

"Will I get my bail money back?" I asked.

"Yes, you will. The orders to release Liam didn't reach the jail before you bailed him out, but he's a free man."

"Oh, dear!" exclaimed June, clasping her throat with a jewel-laden hand. "I might have overplayed my hand."

"If it is any consolation, I think Liam genuinely wanted to examine the necklace as he explained–not steal it."

"What should I do?" asked June, rather put out and looking at each one of us.

Matt offered, "May I make a suggestion? The baby and I are creating too much work for Charles and his daughters. Let me take on Liam. He can work for me, and I'll pay his wages while we stay here. It's a win-win situation for everyone."

June looked at Charles. "Well?"

Charles said to Matt, "I might need him occasionally to help me, if that would be all right."

Matt thrust out his hand. "Done."

Charles laughed and shook Matt's hand. "What a lunatic asylum this house is."

June clapped her hands together. "Yes, but isn't it such fun! That's settled. Tell Liam he can come home, but I shan't speak to him yet. He needs to suffer a bit more as far as I'm concerned."

"I'll jerk a knot in his tail," I replied.

We heard the door open and in walked Liam grinning from ear to ear.

"I suppose you were listening at the door?" I snapped.

"Of course. What good am I as a con man if I don't keep my skills up to snuff?" He turned to Matt. "How may I be of service to you, sir?"

"There's a ton of laundry to do. We use cloth diapers for the baby, so I have the laundry done at my house. I don't use the Big House's facilities for that. Amelia can fill you in on how to handle the cloth diapers properly."

Liam swallowed and nodded, but said nothing.

Lady Elsmere's eyes twinkled at the thought of Liam handling baby poo.

"Then you need to gather my mail. After that, the lawn at my cottage needs to be mowed, and then our rooms here need to be cleaned, especially the bathrooms. I'm afraid the baby is quite messy."

"That will certainly take a lot off my plate," agreed Charles.

"No problem, sir. No problem at all. I'll get right on it. Let me change my clothes first," declared Liam, before pausing in front of June. "I know you are still angry with me, but I adore you still."

June looked the other way.

"Right," moaned Liam before moving to gather the laundry.

"Let me show you our rooms," offered Matt.

"Don't bother, sir. I'll find them. I'll just follow the smell of baby vomit and soiled diapers. And before I forget my manners, congratulations on your baby girl."

"Thank you, Liam. That's all for now."

"Very good, sir." Liam bounded up the servants' stairs to the second floor.

"Do you think he'll be all right?" I asked, trying not to laugh at the absurdity of the situation.

"You should have thought of that before you sprang him from the greybar hotel," sneered June.

"You mean the hoosegow, the clink, the slammer, the pokey, the pen, the joint, Sing Sing . . ."

June protested, "I put Liam there to keep him out of trouble."

"You put him there because he embarrassed you. The hole, the farm, the rock, juvie," I continued.

Matt put his hand over my mouth and pulled me away while saying, "Don't worry. I'll keep an eye on him. If he causes any trouble, I'll send him Josiah's way."

As Matt "escorted" me to my car, we ran into Franklin walking Matt's new friend, the ugly mutt. Franklin looked pained. "See, Josiah. I told you he would eventually make me a dog walker." Franklin sighed, "I can't sink any lower than this."

As Matt pushed me into my car, I yelled, "Don't worry, Franklin. Your status is about to get a boost."

"You mean it?" Franklin broke out into song. *"Grey skies are gonna clear up, put on a happy face . . ."*

Laughing, Matt closed the car door. "Go home, Josiah. You've caused enough commotion today."

It had been a long time since I had seen Matt laugh, so I didn't want to ruin it. I started my car, and waving good-bye, I hurried to the Butterfly. I had to help Eunice prepare for the big gala anyway.

20

Matt and I worked Liam like a one-armed paper hanger. Currently he was unloading food from my car into the kitchen at the Hilltop Manor, while Eunice was counting glasses and bottles of champagne. My job was to open the kitchen door as Liam passed back and forth.

"Thank goodness Hilltop has a commercial kitchen. The food will be piping hot," beamed Eunice as she rushed past me.

"Everything will be wonderful, Eunice. It always is with you."

"Thanks, Josiah," Eunice replied while putting the champagne on ice. "I couldn't have finished the prepping in time if you and Liam hadn't pitched in." She looked up from her task. "Shouldn't you be getting back to the Butterfly to get ready?"

"I thought I was going to help you set up, so I

brought my dress. I can change upstairs."

Eunice stopped what she was doing. "I hired Charles' grandsons to help in the kitchen and serve. Charles has trained them well, and they need the money. They all have girlfriends with expensive tastes."

As she said that, I saw the Dupuy boys pull up in an old El Camino. Hmm. Where did they get that?

"Scoot, Josiah. You look tired."

"Do I?"

"Yes, go home and get some rest before the gala. Everything's under control."

I nodded, but I didn't leave. Instead, I went to speak with Liam.

The conversation between us was strictly private.

21

I never did go back to the Butterfly, my home on the palisades. There was no point. By the time I got home, I would have needed to turn right around and come back. So I gathered my bag and had Liam carry it to one of the guest bedroom suites upstairs. It took me a long time to walk up the flight of steep stairs because my leg was starting to tremble. I guess I had done too much today.

As soon I was ensconced in one of the back bedrooms, I took the room's skeleton key and locked myself in. Then I took a pain pill and lay down, hoping no one would find me. I didn't want to be berated for using the elegant four-poster antique bed for taking a little snooze. You see, I wasn't supposed to be there.

Before long, I fell into a deep sleep. However, my nap was cut short as I was awakened by the sound of someone running through the hall and trying to open my door. Finding it locked, they ran away.

Oh dear! I've been caught. Getting up, I hurried to the window, where I could see that night had fallen and the parking lot was littered with cars. Behind some trees near the old ice house, I saw a figure move. I couldn't tell if it was a man or woman and didn't care. I looked at my watch. Oh, Jumping Jehosaphat! It was 8:45. The gala started at 8 pm. I was beyond fashionably late.

Hurriedly, I threw on my dress, the off-the-shoulder blue chiffon Dior, and blue house slippers. With record speed, I put on makeup and combed my hair. Perusing myself in the mirror, I decided I was passable. Gathering my day clothes and makeup into my bag, I opened the window and threw the bag behind the bushes surrounding the house. I would have Liam collect the bag for me later. Then I straightened the room. After making sure everything was in place, I turned the skeleton key, opened the door slightly, and peered out. Seeing no one about, I walked out and made my way down the servants' staircase.

The kitchen was bustling. Eunice was snapping orders to her crew. I caught Liam's eye as he was heading out with a tray of champagne. He headed over to me, and I was only too happy to accept a glass while whispering to him about my bag in the bushes. He nodded and hurried through the kitchen door.

I followed him to the next room.

An enormous buffet and open bar were set up in the room, which was packed full of attendees filling their plates and chugging down copious amounts of punch and alcohol.

I pushed through the jubilant crowd, greeting friends and acquaintances as I made my way to the enormous ballroom where the exhibit was held. Hearing my name, I turned and spied Franklin waving to me. Beside him stood Matt. Franklin grabbed Matt's arm and navigated through the crowd.

"Good evening," crowed Franklin, dressed in a white dinner jacket with black pants, white shirt, accented by a black bow tie, with his hair slicked back. Matt was dressed in a classic black tuxedo with a red rose boutonnière. He was letting his hair grow out to its former curly glory instead of the nearly bald cut he'd worn when he was so ill. He looked almost like his old self.

Smiling, I said, "You both look gorgeous."

Franklin spun around, showing off his '60s look. "You like? Very James Bond, don't you think?"

"I very much like."

Franklin pointed to Matt. "Look. He asked me to come with him, and I've been taken off dog walking detail. Things are looking up."

"Shut up, Franklin." Matt rolled his eyes, but I could tell he was having a good time.

"Feeling okay?" I asked Matt.

Matt put his arm around my shoulder and squeezed. "The best I've felt in a long time. It wasn't until I got back to Kentucky that I realized how uncomfortable I was living in Meriah's house. It wasn't home, you know. It was hers, and it felt like I was imposing, although I think Meriah needed me during the pregnancy."

"I will grant that Meriah had a lot to deal with–the pregnancy and you being so severely injured. It couldn't have been easy," added Franklin.

Matt looked stunned. "What? You're giving Meriah a compliment?" He shot a grin at Franklin. "Well, wonders will never cease."

"I feel wonderful enough tonight to forgive anyone, even Meriah," laughed Franklin before giving me the once-over. "That is until I see Josiah dressed for this occasion without my advice. I notice you're wearing that tired old Dior again."

"Franklin!" cautioned Matt sternly.

"A Dior is never old," I replied, feeling a little bit peeved. "And I was dressing myself long before you were born, Franklin."

"Why is your face so puffy, Josiah?" inquired Franklin, moving closer and peering into my eyes.

"Really, Franklin," scolded Matt. "You're insulting Josiah and being a boor."

"I'm sorry, Josiah. Except for the swollen cheeks, you look great."

I declared, "Franklin, you sure know how to make a

girl feel good about herself." Angry and fearful Franklin was on to my secret, I turned and melted into the crowd. Over the noise of the crowd, I could hear Matt berating Franklin.

That made me smile.

22

Grabbing another glass of champagne off a passing tray, I wandered into the exhibit, where a pianist was banging away at popular songs from the forties.

"Hey, Toots."

I turned around. There stood Walter Neff wearing a black tuxedo, hair combed (what little there was), freshly shaven, shoes shined, neck free of gold chains, and his fly zipped all the way up. This was a night full of wonders. "Hello, Walter. I didn't know they made tuxedo trousers that short."

Ignoring my remark, Walter said, "You look swell."

That made me feel a little bit peevish, and I reminded myself that I didn't have to be a bitch all the time. "Sorry, Walter. You look very nice, too."

Walter patted his waistcoat. "I know you like to make fun at my expense, but you can't deny that I look like a shiny penny tonight."

I chuckled. "You're so right. Miss Bunny must be rubbing off on you."

Walter elbowed me and winked. "I'm staying at Ravensnest until the case is over. If I play my cards right, maybe I can make this a permanent gig."

"Bunny has terrible taste in husbands, so I think you should fit right in." Dang it. There I go again.

Walter smirked. "You can't goad me tonight, Toots. I've got the world by the tail. Things are finally shakin' my way."

"Speaking of the case."

"Were we?" replied Walter, grabbing an hors 'oeuvre from a passing tray. He popped it into his mouth.

"What's going on?"

"Sorry. Client confidentiality. By the way, have you looked at that journal yet?"

"I told you I wasn't going to do that."

Walter shrugged. "No hard feelings. I'll pick it up next week."

"Please do," I replied, watching Thaddeus McPherson make his way toward us, wearing '20s evening wear complete with tails and white waistcoat.

"Hello, Mrs. Reynolds. Enjoying the gala?"

"Very much. It's a splendid affair."

Walter nudged me.

"This is Walter Neff. Walter, this is Thaddeus McPherson, the man who arranged the exhibit."

Mr. McPherson shook Walter's hand. "Call me Teddy please. Nice to meet you. Hope you are enjoying yourself."

"How did you get all these dames–I mean ladies–to loan their dresses? I don't know much about couture, but I know these rags cost a bundle."

I winced, but kept a smile frozen on my face.

Teddy looked back and forth between Walter and me, probably trying to gauge if Walter was pulling his leg. He decided to take Walter at face value. "It's easy if you know how to ask correctly. Please excuse me. I must tend to my other guests."

I nodded, hoping my cheeks weren't too bright red.

Giving a slight bow, Teddy McPherson disappeared into the crowd.

Scowling, Walter stood on his toes and scanned the crowd. "I wonder where Bunny took off to? She said she was going to the powder room, but she's been gone a long time."

She couldn't take much of you either, I thought. "I've got to work the room myself. Please excuse me."

"If you see Bunny, tell her I'm waitin' on her."

"Will do," I replied, beginning to push my way through the crowd to see my Roberto Capucci dresses. "Excuse me. Pardon. It's a little tight in here, isn't it? So sorry. Oh, hello, nice to see you again. Let's do lunch soon. Hello darling, you look fab. Kiss, kiss. Call me. Coming through."

Halfway through the crowd, I spied Lady Elsmere with Mrs. Dupuy holding court in a corner so friends and well-wishers could line up to congratulate Her Ladyship since she had the greatest number of dresses in the exhibit.

Both ladies were wearing lots of sparkling gems, but June easily won with her diamond tiara. Not only did she look like she had borrowed the Statue of Liberty's crown, she had the same frosty look on her face when her peepers got a fix on me. "Where have you been?" demanded Lady Elsmere. "Did you just get here?"

"I was helping Eunice," I replied. Not the exact truth, but I didn't feel I needed to give an exact account of my whereabouts. "I see that you two are having a great time."

Both Lady Elsmere and Mrs. Dupuy smiled.

"Did you know that dreadful man was working here?" questioned Lady Elsmere.

"I don't know to whom you are referring."

"Don't be impertinent. There he is."

Out of the corner of my eye I saw Liam approach, carefully balancing a tray. He ceremoniously bent down and offered Lady Elsmere and Mrs. Dupuy each a glass of champagne. Mrs. Dupuy took a glass, while Lady Elsmere looked the other way.

"See that I'm still in the doghouse," Liam murmured before moving on.

Hearing a restless crowd stir behind me, I knew I had

better shove off. "I'm off to see my dresses. Talk to you both later. We can compare notes," I said, moving away.

After negotiating the gallery floor, I finally made it to my dresses and whom did I find stationed in front of them? Ellen Boudreaux–my late husband's mistress!

She was with one of her prissy friends, criticizing Brannon for not pinching one of my Capucci dresses before he dumped me for her.

"I don't know why she's crying poor mouth when she could sell one of these dresses and get herself out of debt," harangued Ellen.

"I heard she's in the black since the city settled that lawsuit with her–millions and millions," said her friend.

"What a waste of our tax money," complained Ellen. "Hey, have you got a cigarette? It would be a pity if it was accidentally dropped and burned a hole in the fabric."

I stepped on the train of Ellen's sparkly silver dress and leaned over, whispering in her ear. "This is a non-smoking facility."

Startled, Ellen turned suddenly, which resulted in a sound like fabric ripping. She looked over her shoulder at me, and then the back of her dress. "Get off my gown," hissed Ellen.

"So sorry. Didn't realize that I was standing on your tail–I mean train."

"See if there's a rip," demanded Ellen of her friend.

I moved back to allow her friend to inspect the back of Ellen's dress.

"Just a little tear, easily fixed. Come on. I've got a small sewing kit in my car. We can fix it in a jiffy," she said, tugging at Ellen's arm.

"Yeah, you better take care of that. And one more thing," I said in passing. "If there is any damage to my dresses, I'll make sure you and your friend feel it."

"Feel what?"

"My displeasure, or rather my daughter's. You remember Asa? She'd snatch the pitchfork from the Devil if she was mad enough, and she's counting on inheriting those two dresses in pristine condition."

At the mention of Asa's name, both women blanched.

"Come on," begged her friend. "You've made your point. Let's go."

Ellen let herself be led away by her girlfriend, but not before she shot me a withering glance.

I gave her the finger, subtly, of course. Come on, now. You know why. I hate that woman.

After watching Ellen exit the ballroom, I stood back and listened to people's comments about my dresses.

They were wonderfully displayed on mannequins with moveable parts, and it looked like the dresses were in motion. Combined with accessories, the dresses looked better than they did on me. I had worn the petal dress to a function only once, and the kimono dress had never been seen in public until this exhibit.

I bought the dresses thinking I was going to live a life of parties and good times with Brannon. I hadn't noticed the storm brewing on the horizon. The good times slowly dissolved until there were none, and after Brannon left, the invitations to grand functions dried up. I had nowhere to wear the fabulous dresses, so I was happy that they would be appreciated now for the art they were. The gala attendees seemed mesmerized by them.

"The Capuccis seem to be a hit," chatted Thaddeus, suddenly beside me.

I smiled warmly at him. "Yes, they do. I'm very happy for them."

"Happy for a dress?"

"Happy that they are getting the recognition they deserve, and for the artist who created them."

"I need a break from glad-handing. Would you like to join me on the veranda?"

"That would be lovely."

Teddy offered his arm, which I took, and then escorted me to the veranda. I swear there was a fifteen-degree difference between the outdoors and inside Hilltop Manor.

"This is much better," he said. "The house has been chilling for several days, but it feels like someone turned the AC off."

"Lots of spectators churning up the heat in there. You should be glad the gala is so successful."

"I'm very gratified. I'm hoping to have a record number of attendees."

"Whom did you say is the benefactor of this exhibit again?"

Teddy gave a whisper of a smile. "I didn't."

"Forgive me, but I thought you did."

He shook his head. "No, I'm afraid the information is confidential. Nice try, though. Any special reason you need to know?"

"I don't like secrets. That's all."

Teddy smiled until his dimples showed. "I don't think that's quite true, Josiah. May I call you by your Christian name? I believe you have lots of secrets. It's other people's secrets that you don't appreciate. I hear you're very good at rooting them out."

"Moi?" I gently rested a hand on my chest, trying to present a picture of innocence. "What secrets could I possibly have? I'm an open book."

"Lying doesn't suit you. I thought we were closer than that," Teddy replied, looking intently into my eyes as he sidled closer to me.

I detected cologne, soap, peppermint mouthwash, and the slight tinge of sweat. My heart starting beating faster.

For a moment I thought he was going to bend down and kiss me. Instead, he breathed in my hair and made his way slowly down my neck and shoulders, blowing softly on my skin. Oh, dear!

"I always thought lying suited me quite well," I replied laughing. *Uh-oh. Be careful, Josiah. This man could charm the bloomers off a nun.* "If we're so close, you should call me Josiah."

"Unusual name for a woman—that of a Hebrew king."

"I see you've read your Bible."

"King James version," he replied with a wry smile.

"Of course."

Teddy peered into the ballroom. "I'm so sorry, but I should welcome new guests, so you must excuse me. But before I go, I would like to ask if I might see you—socially."

"I don't know," I answered, somewhat dazed. I wasn't expecting this kind of interest from such a handsome and debonair man and, as usual, acted like a complete dolt.

"I shall come for you tomorrow. Around one o'clock, I should think. If I'm going to be later, I'll ring."

"Let me give you my number."

"I know your number, dear lady, and where you live. You're not the only one with connections." Teddy picked up my hand and lightly kissed it. "Au revoir."

I think I curtsied or something equally stupid. Oh, why couldn't I be a sophisticated dame like Rosalind Russell in *Auntie Mame* instead of Mammy Yokum from *Li'l Abner?*

I watched Teddy saunter into the soft light of the ballroom. Finding a chair, I sat down until I composed my fluttering heart. This was so silly at my age, but I was exhilarated to learn I could still feel . . . you know, feel that spark that goes down to your loins. I thought that after Jake left, that would be the end of that, but now I might have a reprieve.

There is no aphrodisiac like hope.

23

The gala was winding down. I was worn out, but I went into the kitchen to help Eunice clean up. Luckily she had everything under control and shooed me away.

I was wondering where to go when Shaneika strolled in wearing a glittering Chanel sheath with matching headpiece highlighted with ostrich feathers. "Mom, someone spilled their drink on my dress," Shaneika whined.

"Here, baby, let me put this on it," replied Eunice reaching for club soda. "You're the fourth woman tonight to get a spill on your dress."

"Everyone is getting soused and sloppy," complained Shaneika, taking in the kitchen. "Oh, hello Josiah," she said as she laid eyes on me. "Didn't see you when I came in."

"You look marvelous," I gushed. "Just like you stepped out of the Roaring Twenties or an F. Scott Fitzgerald novel."

Shaneika beamed. "This is my great-great grandmother's. Mom is the real owner." She added, "Hurry, Mom, Mike is waiting."

Eunice looked up from patting club soda on Shaneika's dress. "I never liked that era of clothing, so I gave it to Shaneika. I'm too bosomy for that style."

"And your great, great grandmother would be?" I asked, hoping to get an answer.

Shaneika laughed and her mother grinned, but neither said a word.

Darn it. When were those two going to spill about their ancestors?

It had to wait, though, since my left leg was starting to tremble. I had been standing for several hours, and now was going to have to find a seat somewhere, and quickly. Fortunately for me, Liam retrieved a chair, and I gratefully planted my bum on it, while Malcolm brought me a glass of ice water and a small plate of leftover hors d'oeuvres. There weren't many left, but Eunice divided what was left, putting them in Reynolds Wrap and sharing with the staff. There was a happy buzz among the employees while cleaning up.

That is until Walter Neff walked through the swinging kitchen door with a worried look on his face and became a killjoy.

"Toots, is Bunny back here?"

"Bunny still hasn't made contact? Hey, Eunice, have you seen Bunny Witt recently?"

"The President of the United States could have come through and I wouldn't have noticed. I was too busy," Eunice replied, stacking trays.

"Anyone?" called out Walter, anxiously scanning the kitchen staff. "Anyone see a woman in a red dress come through here, or see her anywhere else in this joint?"

Everyone stopped what they were doing and looked questioningly at each other.

"I saw a woman in a red dress with you," asserted Malcolm.

"That was around a little before nine o'clock?"

"I don't know, man. I was too busy to look at the time."

"Did you seen her again, by herself or with someone?" asked Walter.

"Sorry. I wasn't paying attention. I can't say that I did. Besides, there were lots of women in red dresses here tonight."

An alarm bell started to go off in my head. I put my hands on the arms of the chair and lifted myself up.

Walter looked expectantly at the staff, but no one said anything else.

I could see the hope die in his face.

"Malcolm, go find Mr. McPherson and bring him here. If you see Liam, tell him I need him," I ordered.

"He's loading up Mrs. Todd's car, but I'll get him once I find this McPherson guy." Malcolm rushed through the kitchen door.

Eunice brought over a glass of ice water for Walter. "Here, baby. Drink this. Sorry, but it's all we have. Everything's been packed, and the coffee machine is turned off."

Walter gratefully accepted the water and took a long sip. "Thank you. I didn't realize I was so thirsty."

Eunice nodded and said, "Worry takes it out of a person. Always better to drink water when that happens. It fills up the empty places in a person that worry saps."

"Walter, she probably had someone take her home," I suggested.

"I hope that's it, but I have a bad feeling about this. My elbow is twitching and that always means trouble. I knew my luck couldn't last."

"You're such a drama queen," I remarked. "Bunny is probably back at Ravensnest, in bed with a headache."

At that moment, Teddy McPherson strode into the kitchen using the servants' stairs with Malcolm following.

Teddy asked, "This young chap says there's a problem. One of the guests can't be found."

Walter spoke up, "I came with Mrs. Bunny Witt, and I haven't seen her for over a couple of hours."

"Perhaps she is out in the parking lot chatting with other guests?"

"I checked. She's not there," disclosed Walter.

"Perhaps she went home with someone else. Sorry, old man, but that does happen," replied Teddy.

"Possibly, but not likely. I want this house checked or I'm calling the police."

Seeing that Walter was resolute, Teddy acquiesced. "Very well, then. Let's check the garden first. She might have gone for a walk and stumbled. It's not very well lit." He turned his attention to the staff, "Please continue packing. We are to vacate the premises by midnight or we all turn into pumpkins."

There was a slight twitter among the young staff, but Eunice ordered everyone back to work.

In the meantime, Malcolm had found Liam. When Walter and Thaddeus started out the back door, I grabbed Walter's arm. "Liam and I will search upstairs. If she's up there, we'll find her."

Walter gave Liam a quick once-over and nodded. Apparently he recognized a fellow ne'er-do-well when he saw one.

"If this woman is in the building, I'll find her, mate." assured Liam.

Walter quickly muttered "thanks" before racing after Teddy, who was already out the back door.

I said to Liam, "This is so like the silly woman to put everyone to all this trouble. She's at home watching reruns of *Murder She Wrote*."

"Let's make sure of that," replied Liam, heading up the servants' stairs with me following. He stopped suddenly. "Where do you think you're going?"

"I'm going to help you," I replied. "This is an enormous mansion."

"Aye, t'is, but you'll be of no use. Look at yourself with your leg twitching. You'll just slow me down, colleen."

I was feeling a little peaked and was glad someone smacked me down for once. "Malcolm, go with Liam," I barked. "Make sure you check all the bathrooms, closets, and even under the beds. You could hide a brass band under those four-posters."

Happy to be free of the drudgery of cleaning up, Malcolm practically danced up the stairs behind Liam.

I eased back into my chair and waited.

24

The upstairs was searched. No Bunny.

The exhibit rooms were searched. No Bunny.

The garden was searched. No Bunny.

The parking lot was searched. No Bunny.

The remaining cars were searched. No Bunny.

The trunks of the remaining cars were searched. No Bunny.

The cellar was searched. No Bunny.

Walter finally got hold of the farm manager, who went over to the Ravensnest mansion. No Bunny.

Where was Bunny Witt of the Philadelphia Witts?

25

I was becoming alarmed, although I tried not to show it. Chances were Bunny was in a bar, having a drink with a man she met at the gala. While I could applaud her for having the good sense to dump Walter Neff, I was going to brain her for panicking everyone, including Walter Neff.

I sat in my chair by the back door and watched Eunice efficiently restore the commercial kitchen to its former state of sparkling cleanliness, all the time wondering if we were destroying a crime scene.

I am not paranoid!!! Nasty things do happen to people.

Finally, everything was washed, dried, put up, stored, mopped, and disinfected. We had fifteen minutes to spare until midnight.

I went to find Teddy McPherson so he could lock up after us, and found him in the mansion's office with Walter perusing a map of the estate.

"Should we call the police?" asked Teddy, looking strained.

Walter shook his head. "They'll take a statement, but won't start lookin' for her until twenty-four hours is up."

I knocked on the open door.

They both looked up.

"I'm sorry to disturb you, but Mrs. Todd is finished and we would like to leave."

"Of course," replied Teddy, folding the map.

"Walter, Bunny will turn up. You'll see," I said.

"I hope so. I've never had a client just disappear on me," replied Walter, tugging at his droopy bowtie. He looked rumpled and tired.

Teddy grabbed a key. "I'll escort you all to your cars."

"That would be appreciated," I replied.

We met Eunice waiting by the back door. Everyone else had left.

Giving the kitchen one last glance, Teddy, Eunice, and I descended the back steps to the brick sidewalk, while Walter watched us from a window.

Teddy offered to take the serving trays Eunice was carrying. She gratefully handed them over, as they were heavy.

He hurried to the parking lot, where there were only four cars left.

The sidewalk was badly lit, but the full moon was helpful in lighting the brick walkway. There was a slight breeze, and I thought I heard something.

"Did you hear that?" I asked Eunice.

"No. Let's go. This place is creepy after dark."

"It sounded like a shutter slamming against the house or a screen door bouncing on its hinges. Wait! There is goes again. Did you hear it this time, Eunice?"

Walter opened the back door and came out on the back stairs with a flashlight. "Something wrong, Toots?"

"I hear something banging," I called back.

Walter quickly joined us. "Where?"

I pointed over to a group of buildings which included a carriage house, an ice house, and a root cellar.

"I checked those already," confirmed Walter, looking disappointed.

"Did you actually go into them?" I asked.

"I flashed the light in. Just saw a bunch of moldy bricks and cobwebs."

Teddy joined us minus the serving trays, which he must have stored by Eunice's car. "What's happening?"

Walter thumbed toward the group of buildings. "Josiah says she hears something banging. I don't."

"Let's check it out," suggested Teddy. "Mrs. Witt could be injured and signaling for help."

We marched in a tight group over to the buildings. The wind had picked up, creating ominous shadows against the poorly lit pathway.

"There!" I exclaimed, pointing. "It's the side door to the carriage house."

Indeed, the side door was bouncing about on its rusty hinges.

Teddy leaned into the doorway of the carriage house and felt about for a light switch. Suddenly the building was flooded with light, which spilled outside onto the pea gravel path where we stood. Eunice and I quickly went inside the well-lit carriage house.

I now know why ancient man feared the dark. It's menacing.

"Mrs. Witt," called Teddy. "Mrs. Witt, are you here?"

Walter began looking inside a nineteenth-century hansom while Teddy checked underneath a 1954 Packard after looking inside.

There were some antique camelback chests in need of restoration parked in a corner. On impulse, I opened one wondering if I would find some handmade quilts or some forgotten treasure.

"Oh, God!" I squeaked.

"What is it?" asked Eunice, hurrying to my side. She peered down into the chest. "Oh, my Lord."

"Walter!" I called. "Come over here. I just found Bunny Witt of the Philadelphia Witts—and she's dead."

26

"Haven't you retired yet, Goetz?" I asked from the front seat of my car. Beyond Detective Goetz, I could see the coroner lift the bagged body of Bunny Witt into his van. I hadn't much cared for Bunny, but she didn't deserve to be murdered and stuffed into an old trunk.

"The job at the DA's ain't open yet. Waiting for another guy to retire, so I can take his place."

I pursed my lips. "Don't you think that taking this case amounts to a conflict of interest?"

"If I recused myself from every murder where I was acquainted with someone, nothing would ever get investigated. Lexington's a small town."

"You should make an exception where I'm concerned."

"You sure got a big chip on your shoulder, lady. Get over it."

"That's because I'm worried you're going to deep-six me, afraid I might tell that you killed O'nan, but I would never drop a dime on you. You should know that."

"Listen to you. What a drama queen. I guess it never occurred to you that you're in as deep as I am."

"How do you figure?"

"'Cause you never went to the authorities with that information, so now you're an accomplice after the fact. Also, it apparently has never occurred to you that I would just say you paid me to kill him. If you squeal, you go to prison, too."

It took a moment to dawn on me that Goetz was right.

"You know, you're pretty lousy at being grateful to someone who saved your life," he spat out.

"Oh, I'm grateful. I'm just lousy at trusting anyone, especially you.

"If I hadn't taken O'nan out, your daughter would have sooner or later, only you would have been dead by then."

Before I could respond, Walter wandered over and asked, "What are you two whispering about?" Poor Walter. He looked disheveled and bewildered.

"Goetz was asking questions about Mrs. Witt," I replied, wondering if Walter had overheard anything.

"What about my Bunny?" asked Walter.

I stifled the urge to snicker and tried to look sincere. The operative word is "tried."

"She's dead," replied Goetz, brutally.

"I know that," growled Walter. "But how?"

"Won't know until the coroner's report. How was the body discovered?" Goetz got his little notebook and stubby pencil out of his shirt pocket.

"The women were leaving when Toots heard a noise. Mrs. Todd, Mr. McPherson, Toots, and me went to investigate. We found the side door to the carriage house open and banging in the wind."

"Who is Toots?"

"I'm afraid I am," I replied.

Goetz gave Walter a curious look. "Who actually discovered the body?"

"I'm afraid I did," I admitted.

"What made you open the trunk?"

"I thought I might find an antique quilt. I don't know. It was an impulse, I guess."

"So you go looking for a missing person and you get sidetracked looking for an old quilt?"

"I know. It sounds terrible."

"What happened after you found the body?"

"I slammed the lid of the trunk shut, and Mr. McPherson called the police."

"If Bunny Witt was missing during the gala, why didn't you call the police earlier?"

Walter intervened, "Because I wasn't really sure she was missing. She could have left with someone. I didn't want to cause Mrs. Witt any embarrassment by being an alarmist. People hire me to keep things quiet."

"You told one of my officers that you were working for Mrs. Witt."

"Yes. She hired me to investigate whether or not she had a stalker."

"Who brought her here?"

"I did," replied Walter, wearily rubbing his forehead with his thumb.

"When was the last time you saw her?"

"Around 9:15, I think."

"What about you, Mrs. Reynolds?"

"I got here around 5 pm."

"Why so early?"

"I was helping Mrs. Todd prep."

"You with her all that time?"

"No. I went upstairs around 6:45 and took a nap."

Goetz raised an eyebrow as he jotted down the information. "Did you have permission to use the upstairs bedrooms?"

"No."

"Sounds like you. What time did you join the gala?"

"I'm not sure. I fell into a deep sleep and was awakened by someone running through the hallway and trying to open my door."

"Why your door?"

"I don't know, but when I went out into the hall, I noticed all the doors to the upstairs rooms were closed. When I first went upstairs they were all standing open with the skeleton keys in their locks."

"Were the keys in the doors when you went downstairs?"

"I didn't notice any keys when I went downstairs, but I can't swear to that."

"You said someone was running through the hall?"

"Yes."

"Not walking fast, but running?"

"I can't be sure. I was coming out of a deep sleep, but she was moving fast enough that I heard the rustle of a gown."

Goetz stopped taking notes and peered down at me. "So it was a woman?"

"I thought so. My first inclination was that she was looking for a restroom."

Goetz turned to Walter. "Was Mrs. Witt wearing a dress that would rustle?"

Walter shrugged. "She was wearing a dress from some sort of stiff fabric. I don't know what you call it."

"Bunny was wearing a red dress that had a sequined bodice with a taffeta skirt. The skirt would make noise when she walked," I interjected. "I noticed the dress when I opened the trunk."

"Anything else?"

I thought for a moment. "You'll find footprints underneath the window of the room I was staying in. I threw my bag out the window," I said, leaving Liam out of the picture. He didn't need further attention from the police.

"Why didn't you take it out through the house like a normal person?"

"Because I didn't want anyone to know I had been napping upstairs. Look, I'm guilty of using an antique bed without permission, but that's all. I had nothing to do with Bunny Witt's demise. Can I go home now? I'm bushed."

"Yeah, but Mr. Neff, I need you to come to the morgue and identify the body. Mrs. Witt doesn't seem to have any kinfolk."

"She had a personal assistant who might have come to town for the gala," I said.

Looking miffed, Walter claimed, "If that's true, I haven't seen her, and Mrs. Witt didn't mention anything about any personal assistant,"

"Got a name for this assistant?" asked Goetz, furiously writing everything down.

I shook my head.

Goetz mocked, "Of course not."

"Lady Elsmere might know," I suggested.

"I'll give her a call. Also, I want a look in your bag before you leave."

I reached around, grabbing my bag from the backseat of the car and held it out.

Goetz stuck his notebook and pencil in his coat pocket before putting on gloves.

"Hurry or I'm going to drop this. It's heavy," I pleaded.

Goetz grabbed the bag and pulled the zipper carefully. Walter crowded in behind him so he could peek as well.

All Goetz found was a damp toothbrush, my dirty work clothes, a pair of tennis shoes, makeup kit, and a hairbrush. "Okay, you can go," he said.

I threw the bag into the backseat again and started the car. I drove very slowly past the coroner's van and multiple police cars with their lights flashing violently into the dark of the cool night.

Looking into my rearview mirror, I saw Teddy McPherson speaking with Goetz, who once again had his notebook out.

I'm ashamed to say my last thought leaving the parking lot was not of poor, dead Bunny.

I wondered if Teddy was still going to call on me the next day.

27

Matt and I accompanied Lady Elsmere to Bunny Witt's funeral.

The crowd was smaller than expected. I guess Bunny's friends were in New York, where she spent most of her time.

Standing near the casket was a blond woman in her thirties receiving the few people who had bothered to attend this dreary affair. She had an air of authority about her.

Lady Elsmere passed her to view Bunny, but Matt and I stopped to introduce ourselves.

"Hello. I'm Josiah Reynolds and this is Matthew Garth. We're so sorry for your loss."

The woman had reddish, puffy eyes as if she had been crying recently. "I'm Emma Fisher. I am—I mean—I was Mrs. Witt's personal assistant. I know who you are, Mrs.

Reynolds. Mrs. Witt told me how you were helping her with this dreadful business of a stalker. If you have a few minutes after the funeral, I would very much like to speak with you."

"I'm not sure how long we will be staying," I replied, pointing to Lady Elsmere bending over the coffin and patting Bunny's hand.

Seeing Lady Elsmere looked frail indeed, Ms. Fisher said, "Of course. Here's my card. Please call me, Ms. Reynolds, and soon. I need to speak with you."

Curious, I took the card and nodded. "I'll call you this evening, if that is all right."

"That would be fine."

"Please excuse my friend," I said, referring to Lady Elsmere. "She was a dear friend of Bunny's mother, and this death has hit her hard."

Emma Fisher shot a quick look at Lady Elsmere. "So that must be June Webster, the woman Mrs. Witt was staying with? I should have realized. Please excuse me. I would like to personally thank her for taking Mrs. Witt under her wing during her time of need."

Matt and I nodded and retreated to a back room in the funeral home where there were refreshments. I needed something to drink and perhaps a cookie to lift my spirits. Seeing Bunny in a coffin had unnerved me. Perhaps I should have taken her situation more seriously.

Jumping Jehosaphat! There was no doubt about it.

In a corner sat a glum Walter Neff. He stood when he saw me.

"Pardon me, Matt. I should speak with Walter."

"I'm going to drink this bottle of water, and then I'll go check on June. Take your time."

I crossed the room to Walter and sat beside him.

"How you holding up, Walter?"

Walter shook his head. "I keep going over that night and I can't make sense of it."

"I think someone lured Bunny out and then killed her."

"But why? Nothing was stolen. We found her purse. Nothing was taken, and she was wearing all her jewelry when she was found."

"Maybe your angle is all wrong. Let's say robbery wasn't the reason. What else might have triggered her death?"

"I've checked her exes. They all have alibis. Hell, they weren't even in the state."

"That doesn't mean that they couldn't have hired someone."

"Yeah, but what's the motive?"

"Revenge?"

"She either gave them a big check up front when she divorced them, or was paying alimony. Upon her death the alimony payments stopped. There was no incentive there. Rule the husbands out."

"It's got to do with this stalker business then," I insisted.

Just as Walter started to say something Emma Fisher came into the room with Lady Elsmere clutching her arm for support. At the sight of Ms. Fisher, he blanched. Instead of finishing what he was about to say, Walter mumbled, "I'll holler atcha later," and fled the room.

I studied Ms. Fisher as she watched Walter leave. She didn't seem pleased to see him at the funeral home, but I didn't have time to analyze why, because June reached for my hand.

"Take me home, Josiah," said she in a raspy voice. "I've had enough of death today."

Matt rushed over and took June's arm, escorting her to the Bentley.

Emma Fisher called after me, "Don't forget to call me, Mrs. Reynolds. It's imperative that I talk with you."

"I will, but I must go now. Lady Elsmere seems to be very upset. I need to be with her."

Ms. Fisher nodded and went back into the room where her former employer was laid out in a very ornate, copper-colored coffin.

I looked back to see Emma Fisher wipe a tear from her face as she walked away.

At least there was someone who had truly cared for our Miss Bunny.

That's more than many of us get when we die.

28

I met Emma Fisher at the Chevy Chase Inn, a local watering hole in the Chevy Chase section of town. She was waiting for me in a back booth.

I ordered a Virgin Bloody Mary before joining her.

"Thank you for coming," Emma said.

"No problem. This place is not too far from home. Everything done for Bunny?"

Emma took a sip of her Long Island Iced Tea. "Mrs. Witt was interred next to her mother in the Lexington Cemetery." She reached inside her purse for a tissue when tears clouded her eyes. "Next month I'll return to New York for a memorial service. That's where most of her friends are. I was surprised that so few people showed up for Mrs. Witt's funeral. Shocked, actually."

"You seemed to be devoted to her."

"Yes, I was. Mrs. Witt was a very kind woman. Most

people did not realize that about her. She came off as kind of frivolous, I know, but Mrs. Witt was a sincerely a good-hearted woman."

"If you say so," I replied. "How long had you worked for Bunny?"

"Eleven years. Next September would have made it twelve."

"Was she a good employer?"

"She was very demanding about certain things, but Mrs. Witt paid above scale. This suit I'm wearing–it's hers. I could never afford something this expensive. When she was tired of an outfit, she gave to me. Sometimes she had never even tried it on before she gave it to me." Emma took a sip of her drink. "When my father took ill, Mrs. Witt paid all his hospital bills. I didn't even know about it until I went to talk to the hospital about establishing monthly payments. The clerk told me all my father's bills had already been paid in full by Mrs. Witt."

"That was indeed generous," I agreed, surprised. "What was it that you wanted to see me about, Ms. Fisher?"

"Did you ever discover who was stalking Mrs. Witt?"

"I was not able to. That's why she hired Walter Neff."

"That odious little man," spat Emma. "I need to close Ravensnest, but he absolutely refuses to leave. He says he's staying put until he solves the case. I'm going to start an eviction process if he doesn't leave by this weekend. Do you know who recommended him? I'd like to wring her neck."

"I haven't the foggiest," I lied. "You don't think Walter Neff had anything to do with Bunny's murder, do you?"

"It seems he was the last person to see her alive. Why not?"

"Because there was no profit in it for him. Walter Neff doesn't do anything unless it benefits him."

Emma's eyes narrowed. "How would you know that about him?"

Ooops! Trying to change the subject, I asked, "Ms. Fisher, who does benefit from Bunny's death? Have you seen her will?"

"I'm the executrix. Her exes, including a couple of favorite former boyfriends, get a million each. Theda Finkelstein, her cook, gets two million, as do I. I also get the New York apartment with an annuity for maintenance fees if I want it. The bulk of her estate will be liquidated and will fund a philanthropic foundation."

"Who is to head this foundation?"

Emma's cheeks reddened a little bit. "Mrs. Witt wanted me to head the foundation."

I leaned against the back of the bench seat. "I see. How long ago was the will written?"

"Last year. Please don't think I encouraged her, Mrs. Reynolds. I didn't even know until Mrs. Witt's lawyer recently informed me."

"The will has already been read?"

"No. Not officially. He called to brief me just after Mrs. Witt's death. Unless her murder is solved quickly, the probate will not move forward for now."

"Hmm."

"I'm frightened, Mrs. Reynolds. Someone was out to get Mrs. Witt. I'm worried that whoever was after her may well come after me next."

"You believe it has something to do with the terms of the will?"

"I don't know what it has to do with. It all started when she gave an interview to a reporter in London about that silly tale of her aunt getting jewels from some raja in India."

Emma really had my attention now. I leaned forward. "When was this?"

"About a year ago. No, not quite that long ago, but about. It was only a paragraph in the story about her family, but the ruckus it stirred up in London—it was horrible. Mrs. Witt was even contacted by the Indian consulate, who asserted any jewels given were the rightful property of the Indian government and must be returned."

Emma had grown extremely animated, gesturing with trembling hands. "The London apartment was ransacked. Goodness, what a mess. Someone even slashed open her mattress, and punched holes in the walls to search behind the plaster. It was too much. I packed our bags and we got out of there pronto."

"She never mentioned that to me. Wait." I thought for a moment. "As a matter of fact, she did. Bunny said her apartment had been searched in London, and that's why she was in New York. She made it sound rather trivial."

"It wasn't, I assure you. It was terrifying."

"Walter Neff told the police he wasn't aware that you were in town. In fact, he remarked that he didn't even know you existed," I said.

"I was staying at Mrs. Witt's apartment in town."

"But why not stay at Ravensnest?"

"I don't know. Mrs. Witt just told me to stay at the apartment in town."

"Who else was staying at Ravensnest?"

"There is a farm manager and a housekeeper, but they don't live on the farm. The only people staying at Ravensnest were Mrs. Witt and Walter Neff, what little good that did her."

"Have you spoken to Detective Goetz?"

"Yes. Several times."

"What does he say?"

Emma threw up her hands. "Nothing. Just says he's working on the case."

"He's a very good detective. If this case can be solved, the identity of the murderer will be discovered. Goetz will root him out." I paused for a moment. "Ms. Fisher, I still don't understand why you felt you needed to talk to me?"

"I thought you might know something that the police don't. Mrs. Witt did turn to you. She trusted you. I'm grasping at straws, I know."

"Ms. Fisher, please believe me. I don't know who killed Bunny or who was causing her such distress, but let me give you a piece of advice. I would go back to New York, double the locks on your apartment, get a security system, change your phone number, and hunker down until this is over. I don't know if you are in danger, but why take the chance? Get out of Lexington. Get out today."

Ms. Fisher's face drained of color. She hurriedly threw a twenty on the table and fled the bar.

I hoped I had put the fear of God into Emma Fisher. If someone was out to get her, it would take all of her strength and cunning to elude him.

I oughta know.

29

I confess I was a little rattled when I left the Chevy Chase Inn. Maybe I should have had a real Bloody Mary after all.

Did I believe Emma Fisher was in danger, and that she acutally had cared for Bunny Witt? Everyone I had talked with about Bunny thought she was a selfish twit. Did Bunny have hidden depth after all? It was hard to fathom. I didn't believe Emma's story–plain and simple. Call it my gut rumbling. I think she was fishing.

Okay. I will accept the fact that I'm paranoid. I will agree with you that I have turned into a cynical woman, given to sarcasm and bad manners, but I'm not heartless. I just didn't believe the "I'm frightened, Auntie Em, I'm frightened" speech.

As things turned out I should have. I should have done more, but I didn't.

But what else could I have done? I gave her good advice.

Emma just failed to take it.

30

I was completely exhausted and went straight to bed. I didn't want to hear any more about Bunny Witt. Let Walter Neff and Goetz sort it out.

I was in a deep slumber when something awakened me. Sitting up in bed, I listened.

Baby was barking by the front door. He was so loud, the sound had echoed through the house to my back bedroom. Now Baby growls at many things during the night that he deems dangerous—cats chewing on his ears, a raccoon getting a drink of water out of the pool, a deer rambling across the driveway—but he rarely barks at night. It's not the English Mastiff way.

I got up, grabbed my Taser, and went to the front door, turning on all the outdoor lights. In a coat closet just inside the front door, I have monitors for my many surveillance cameras. I checked the camera by the electronic front gate. Nothing. I checked the camera for Matt's house. Nothing.

"False alarm, buddy. Let's go back to bed."

Baby leaned against me and whimpered.

"It's okay, Baby. Nothing's out there. Come on. Let's go back to bed."

I started back to my room with Baby padding behind me when the telephone rang. My heart dropped. Phone calls in the middle of the night were rarely a good thing. I almost didn't answer it, but the phone kept ringing and ringing, making Baby crazy with its noise. He kept walking in circles while looking up at me anxiously.

Finally gathering my courage, I answered, "Hello?"

"Josiah? Josiah, this is Charles."

"Charles, please don't tell me something has happened to June."

"No. No. Nothing like that, but someone broke into the Big House tonight. If it hadn't been for that mangy dog I rescued, we never would have known someone was in the house. Apparently our alarm system was disabled, but that dog took a chunk out of whoever broke in.

"June is awfully torn up," he continued. "She wants to know that you're okay. I'm sending Liam and Malcolm to your place to search the grounds and stay the night."

"Thank you, Charles, but I don't think that's necessary."

"She's not going to take no for an answer," replied Charles heatedly, which meant he agreed with his employer.

It seemed I was outnumbered. "Is everyone okay?"

"We think so, but whoever was in the house opened the door to the baby's room. The dog was sleeping by the baby's crib and just tore into the guy. Matt rushed in and saw a man run down the staircase with the dog chasing after him."

"Chalk one up for the hound."

There was silence on the phone.

"What's wrong?"

"The mutt followed the intruder outside, and now we can't find him."

"That's not good. Listen, I've got a friend who has a trained Bloodhound. Let me call right now and get that dog. By the time she gets here with her hound, it will be light, and we can search for your courageous mutt."

Charles paused again, as if wondering what was the right thing to do.

"She owes me a favor. Surely a dog that chased an intruder out of the house deserves a thorough search. What would take us humans hours to cover will take this dog minutes."

"Make the call, Josiah," said Charles, before hanging up.

31

Baby knew something was up. He was such a pill while I was dressing that I gave him some sleeping medication wrapped in roast beef to make him take a nap.

Tiptoeing out of the Butterfly, I waited at the gate for my friend for forty-five minutes. The sky was pitch black. It looked like someone had splashed printer's ink across it. What do they say about the night being the darkest before the dawn?

Before the first light peeked over the hills, my friend arrived in her pickup truck with Sami, her Bloodhound, in the passenger's seat. Sami didn't look too pleased when I scooted him over so I could climb into the pickup. Starting with my jeans, he snorted and sniffed all the way up to my hair. Since Sami's nose was so sensitive, he probably knew more about me than I did by the time he reached the top of my head.

He stuck his cold, wet nose against my neck and left it there.

"Uh, what does he want?" I asked.

"Sami's saying howdy."

"Sami's pressing me into the door. I've got a handle sticking me in the ribs."

"Then I guess you'll stay like that till we get there," replied Sami's handler, pulling into the Big House's driveway and driving to the back of the house where Matt told me he'd be waiting.

He was standing along with Liam, Charles, and his four grandsons—all seven loaded for bear.

Matt opened the door, which was good since I couldn't reach the handle. He helped me out while Sami's handler barked a command and put a leash on him—Sami, not Matt.

"Thank you very much," said Matt, thrusting out his hand. "I'm Matt Garth. I'm sure Josiah has given you all the details."

"Hazel's my name, Hazel Mott. Pleased ta meetcha. This here's Sami," Hazel replied, hardily shaking his hand. "Time's awastin'. You got something that belonged ta the dog we're lookin' fer?"

Matt handed Hazel a stuffed pig. "This is his chew toy."

"That's good. What's the dog's name?"

"I don't know. I hadn't got around to naming him," Matt replied sheepishly.

"That ain't good. Dog's gotta have a name," Hazel spat out.

Charles piped in, "He's a stray I found several weeks ago."

"That's enough time for him to bond," said Hazel allowing Sami to sniff the chew toy. "Don't worry, Mr. Garth. Sami will find your dog if he's still around." Hazel turned her attention to Sami. "Sami, find. Sami, find."

The Bloodhound immediately put his magnificent proboscis to the ground and began sniffing. Sami zigzagged around the yard in what appeared to be a random fashion with Hazel in tow. He barked several times and began pulling on the leash.

"Sami's locked on to a scent!" cried Hazel as she started running with him. "Ain't he sumthin'?"

The four grandsons raced after Hazel and Sami while Matt and Liam followed at a slower pace. They ran through the nearest horse pasture, and then behind the breeding barn where I lost sight of them.

"Let's go upstairs," suggested Charles. "We can watch from the widow's walk."

We took the elevator up to the second floor, where Charles pulled down the stepladder to the widow's walk. We both cautiously climbed up.

The air was still very cool, so I wrapped my arms around me. I could see farm workers arriving as the sun began to peek over the hills, with mist from the river filling the valleys in between. Several police cars pulled into the driveway and parked at the front door.

Charles threw his arm out and pointed, "There they are! They're heading for the river!"

"The intruder must have come by boat," I suggested.

"Daddy! The police are here. They want to talk with you," called Amelia, foot on the first rung of the ladder.

"Coming," answered Charles. He climbed down first and then helped me navigate down the rungs. "Where are they?" Charles asked.

"I put them in the front parlor," replied Amelia, looking worn out.

"I'll take care of this. How's Miss June?"

"I got her settled finally. She was very upset that someone broke into the house."

"Go back to bed. If she rings, your mother will see to her."

Amelia looked grateful. "Thanks, Daddy. Bess is in the kitchen making coffee." Nodding good-bye, Amelia quietly disappeared through the door to June's massive suite, where she occupied the nurse's room.

Charles turned and took the stairs, while I went to the first floor on the elevator. Once downstairs, I followed him into the kitchen where Bess was setting up a tray of coffee and cinnamon rolls for the police.

Satisfied with the tray, Bess nodded to her father who picked it up and took it to the waiting policemen in the front parlor.

I sipped on hot coffee at the kitchen table while Bess worked in silence. I could tell her nerves were as frayed as mine.

Several minutes later, three policemen scrambled through the kitchen and out the back door while hastily tipping their hats to us.

I assumed Charles had told them about the Sami searching the grounds and they were hurrying to catch up to the Bloodhound. Peering down the hall, I saw another policeman go up the stairs to the second floor.

Bess stopped to look out the window as she dried her hands on her apron. "They'll be hungry when they get back. I'm gonna make eggs and sausage biscuits for them. You think they'll like that?"

"Uh, let me think, Bess. Men turning down egg and sausage biscuits? Hmmmmm–not going to happen, but I think you should make what's easiest for you. You've had a rough four hours."

"Do you think they'd like ham better?" Not waiting for an answer, Bess turned on the oven and gathered the ingredients to make homemade biscuits. "This will just take a second."

Realizing that Bess was not listening to me, but was in her own safe world of flour, sweet butter, and buttermilk, I continued to gaze out the window and sip on my coffee, not making a sound.

The house was silent except for the ticking of the grandfather clock in the main hallway and the comforting sound of Bess mixing biscuit dough ingredients with her hands. She efficiently rolled out the dough so she could cut it with her round cookie cutter and place the circles on her baking pan.

I watched Bess work smoothly, and with the confidence that only cooks born with her expertise could muster. Bess was an artist with food.

She put the baking pan in the oven and began frying sausage patties. "I'll cook the eggs when I see them coming back. I don't want them overdone. Ruins the flavor," she said to no one in particular.

Out of the corner of my eye, I saw something move around the breeding barn. I sighed. It was only the workers taking the mares out to the pastures.

Fishing through the cabinets, Bess got out several stainless steel bowls and began filling them with water.

"What are those for?" I asked.

Bess shot me a big grin. "Those dogs will be thirsty and hungry. The first biscuit sandwiches will go to them."

"I thought you didn't like dogs."

"I don't like them in my kitchen, but I like dogs. It's your dog I don't like. Can't stand the drool. I don't understand why you keep that filthy animal, Josiah. He stinks to high heaven."

"I keep him because he took a bullet for me. I owe it to Baby to make a comfortable home for him."

Bess twisted her mouth in a comical way. "I guess so, if you put it that way."

I chuckled, "Yep, a person can overlook lots of faults in a pet who took a bullet for her, and Baby doesn't smell that bad."

"Then there is something wrong with your sniffer."

"He's got a good heart."

"I hope so, because that eating and pooping machine doesn't have anything else to recommend him."

"You're starting to hurt my feelings, Bess."

Bess pointed out the window and turned toward me. "Look, the men are back. DADDY! DADDY! THE MEN ARE BACK!"

Charles and the officer upstairs rushed to the kitchen and joined Bess and me on the back patio.

I don't think I breathed until I saw Hazel and Sami. Hazel waved. Behind her marched the four grandsons looking tired and sweaty.

Where were Matt and Liam?

"Did you find the dog?" yelled Charles.

Malcolm pointed behind him. Into view strode Matt with Liam beside him carrying a bundle. It wasn't moving.

Oh, dear. Was the mutt dead?

I rushed into the yard to meet Matt. "What happened? Where are the policemen?"

Matt waved me away as he plopped down in a patio chair. "Let me catch my breath, will ya?" He was breathing heavily and his color was a deep red.

Liam hurried into the kitchen with his bundle.

"Was that the dog?"

"Josiah, I need to rest a bit. I'm out of shape. Go inside. Liam will explain everything."

I reluctantly left Matt and hurried to the kitchen. It was crowded with the men and Hazel, all gulping down hot coffee and stuffing their faces with warm blackberry muffins and sweet butter while Bess was frantically frying eggs for her biscuits.

But where were Liam and the dogs?

I opened the door to the mud room, where Sami was happily slurping water and Liam was in a corner wrapping something furry in a blanket.

"Did you find him?"

"Aye. That Bloodhound went right to him. He was huddled in a little ball under a sycamore tree. With his coloring as camouflage, we would have passed by him, but that hound," he said, pointing at Sami, "found him. T'is a miracle."

"Is he hurt?"

"I think someone has stomped on him. Charles is getting the car so we can take the dog to the vet for X-rays. He's a mighty lucky doggie. Yes, he is," cooed Liam, rubbing the dog's head.

A tongue reached tentatively out of the blanket and licked Liam's hand. I breathed a sigh of relief. The mutt was going to be okay.

Charles popped his head in the door. "Ready, Liam?"

"Aye. I've got him swaddled nice and warm."

"Let's go then. Matt's already in the car."

Liam gently lifted the bundle and followed Charles while I opened doors for him. Following them, I watched the Bentley move down the driveway and out of sight.

As I walked back, I noticed a new car in the front driveway. It looked like Goetz's car. What could he be doing here?

I let myself in the front door and followed voices coming from the kitchen. There stood Hazel, happily snacking on an egg and sausage biscuit, cutting up with Charles' grandsons. Apparently she had grandsons of her own, and was asking questions about sports, college picks, and proposed majors. The boys basked happily in the attention.

Sitting at the kitchen table was Goetz, also eating an egg sausage biscuit with a glass of milk at his elbow.

"I didn't know you handled home invasions as well," I jabbered, not really expecting an answer.

"Heard about the commotion on the police radio and decided to check it out for myself. The boys are still combing the back of the property. Apparently the perp came by boat. Must have been in good shape. It takes a lot to scramble up and down those riverbanks."

"Also knew how to disable a security system," I added.

"Good thing there was a dog in the house."

"Tell me about it." I paused and watched Goetz take a sip of his milk. "Why are you really here?"

Goetz wiped his mouth with a linen napkin

embroidered with June's monogram. "Wanted to see if Walter Neff was the intruder."

"Walter? I don't think Walter is in good enough shape to pull this caper off, let alone hightail it back to a boat with a dog nipping at his buttocks. And besides, why would he?"

"Do you know where our boy Walter might be, Toots?" mocked Goetz.

I leaned forward in my chair and whispered, "Why do you want to know?"

Goetz folded the napkin carefully and laid it on the table before he whispered, "Because I'm going to arrest him for the murder of Emma Fisher. She was found strangled in Mrs. Witt's apartment this morning."

32

I sat stunned, staring at Goetz. The buzz of the people happily chatting in the kitchen seemed to fade in the distance. At last I roused myself to say, "Let's go into the dining room where we can have some privacy." I picked up my cup and went into the dining room with Goetz following.

Sitting at the massive mahogany dining table, I had to catch my breath. Emma Fisher's death was quite a shock.

Goetz waited patiently while I recovered.

"I met with Ms. Fisher last night at the Chevy Chase Inn."

"What did you two discuss?"

"She was concerned that whoever was after Bunny Witt might be after her as well. She wanted to know if I knew anything. I cautioned Ms. Fisher that if she was concerned, she should leave town. Go back to New York."

"Then what happened?"

"She rushed out. That's all I know."

"What about Walter Neff's involvement in this?"

"You can't be serious. Walter's no murderer. What would be his motive?"

"I hear Ms. Fisher couldn't get Neff to move out of Ravensnest, and was in the process of having him evicted."

I guffawed. "Look, I find Walter Neff to be an odious little man, but I can't believe he would kill a woman over something so ridiculous. Walter is used to being thrown out of places. He wouldn't take an eviction personally."

"So you haven't seen him?"

"Not since Bunny Witt's funeral."

"How was Neff's demeanor at the service?"

"He was very down. Walter felt he had failed Bunny."

"I understand Emma Fisher was the principal beneficiary of Mrs. Witt's estate. Perhaps she killed Mrs. Witt to get the money, and Neff killed her in revenge," Goetz suggested.

"If—if—if. I'll tell you a what-if. If Walter thought Emma Fisher had something to do with Bunny Witt's death, he would have blackmailed her for money—not killed her. Walter is all about money. That's his holy grail."

"We'll see about that." Goetz stood. "If he contacts you, call me. Regardless of what you say, I think I'm right."

Goetz gave me one last glance before he strode out the door into the hall.

I sat at the dining table for some time, thinking about the case. Oh, that poor girl. Why hadn't she left Lexington like I told her? Strangled! Horrible, simply horrible!

33

Several days later, I was checking my bees when I heard a truck approach on the gravel driveway. Hopping into my golf cart, I chased down the sound.

I found a flatbed truck delivering a Bobcat to Matt's little shed he called a home. The yard was littered with new lumber.

Matt was busy directing the truck, which was backing up.

I waited patiently until the Bobcat was firmly on the ground and then asked, "What's going on, Matt?"

Matt swung around and beamed. "I'm expanding the cottage. Adding a new master bedroom and bath."

"That's a good idea. With a new baby, the house is too small. Will the nurse take over your current bedroom?"

Matt laughed. "The nurse packed up yesterday and should be basking in the glow of the LA smog as we speak."

"Why? I thought she was working out quite well."

"She decided Kentucky was too wild. I believe the exact word she used was uncouth. She said she was going back to where people were more civilized."

"We do take some getting used to. Who's taking care of the baby?"

"Mrs. Dupuy, until I can find permanent child care." Matt gave me a cursory glance. "I guess you wouldn't want to . . ."

"Don't even think it. I raised one kid who turned out to be a sociopath. I'm not raising another."

"But we love Asa. She may be a sociopath, but she's our sociopath. Just thought I ask." Matt gave me a naughty smirk.

"You look better, Matt. You've gained weight."

"I feel better." He thought for a moment. "I'm going back to work part-time. I think I told you."

"Did you? Can't remember. So much is going on."

"I need to start pulling my own weight again."

"How long will you be staying at the Big House?"

"Until the renovations are complete, at least. Miss June feels more secure with me in the house."

"Are you sure it's not your dog that makes her feel safe?"

"I do think it's more the dog than me, but she is too polite to say so."

"What did you end up naming him?"

"He's a she. The vet had to shave all her fur off so he could look for puncture wounds. He turned out to be female, and I named her Ginger. Get it? Because her coat is a reddish brown."

"I'll try to remember. Ginger, huh?"

"It suits her."

"She okay?"

"A couple of broken ribs, like we thought. The bastard must have kicked her, but she's resting fine now. Bess is feeding her boiled chicken and made a nice bed for Ginger by the back door, so she doesn't have too far to travel to potty."

"Bess has had a change of heart, I see."

"I don't understand why the intruder went into the baby's room."

"Maybe he got confused. Thought he was going into June's suite."

"Maybe, but I'm sleeping in the baby's room until this maniac is caught. Liam has relieved Amelia at night, and is sleeping in the nurse's room."

I laughed. "I knew June couldn't stay mad at Liam for very long. Are they lovebirds again?"

"Not quite, but it's moving in that direction. I'm trying to get as much work out of Liam as possible before June reclaims him."

"I'll let you get back to it. Glad to see you're feeling so much better, Matt."

But Matt didn't reply. He was too busy telling the truck driver where he wanted the Bobcat.

While I was watching Matt, the realization came to me that he wouldn't have much time for me in the future. A baby sucks up all of a person's energy.

It was time for me to ease out of Matt's life. I suddenly felt a piercing sense of loss, but it was only right. Let Matt have his day in the sun.

I had had mine.

34

There was an unfamiliar English roadster in the driveway when I got back to the Butterfly. I'm not much of a car buff, but even I admired this vintage dark green beauty. It had spoked wheels, a silver racing stripe, the steering wheel on the right side. Eunice must have buzzed it in when I was in the bee yard.

Walking into the foyer, I stripped off my bee suit and hung it up. Hearing voices in the great room, I made a beeline, (Get it? Beeline), for it.

To my surprise, there sat Eunice conversing with Teddy McPherson.

I guess the shock showed on my face. I hadn't heard from him since the night of the gala, and that was weeks ago.

"Hello," I managed to say without sounding too petulant. He might have forgotten his promise to call on me, but I certainly hadn't.

Teddy McPherson rose as soon as he saw me. "Dear Josiah. So glad to see you." He rushed to give me a kiss on the cheek.

I flinched a little.

"Isn't it wonderful that Mr. McPherson has come to pay us a visit!" gushed Eunice, obviously enthralled.

Teddy led me to a chair. "I'm so sorry I didn't call first, but I wanted to apologize for my appalling behavior."

"Look at the wonderful flowers he brought," chirped Eunice, pointing to my Nakashima table.

I glanced across the room. There was, indeed, a stunning pink and white floral arrangement on the dining table. It must have cost a small fortune. "It's very nice. Thank you."

Eunice gave me a curious look. She had expected me to be thrilled with arrangement since I adore flowers.

Seeing I was less than happy to see Teddy McPherson, Eunice announced, "I'm going to make some lemonade."

"That would be splendid," encouraged Teddy. "I would love some."

Eunice hurried to the kitchen.

When she disappeared, Teddy sat in a chair next to me. "You don't seem pleased to see me, Josiah. I know. I know. That's why I'm here. I've behaved abominably. I knew a simple apology over the phone would not suffice, so here I am to take my lashes–so flog away."

"You stood me up," I vented.

"Yes, I did."

"And you never called."

"That's true," agreed Teddy. "But then a woman on my watch had been brutally murdered, so I was somewhat preoccupied talking to the police, my lawyer, the lawyer of Hilltop Manor, newspaper reporters, my benefactor, and various nondescript people ringing me up and asking about the events that night. This does not include the charming Detective Goetz taking my fingerprints, absconding with my tux from that night, and subjecting me to a polygraph test. When I didn't call, I thought you would have understood that I was under the gun."

I felt the heat rise up my neck to my cheeks, but I was not going to give in so easily. I don't know why I was behaving like this, but I felt I needed to keep a wall between me and this smooth-talking, charming English gent. "I see."

He leaned forward, staring into my eyes. "Am I forgiven? Please say yes. Let's start anew. I'm here with my chariot to sweep the fair damsel to a wonderful lunch in the beautiful Bluegrass countryside."

I looked down at my dirty hands and torn pants. "It's past lunchtime."

"Then we'll make it an early dinner. How about it? Game?"

Eunice entered with a pitcher of lemonade and glasses.

"Ah, the lovely Eunice. I'm trying to talk Josiah into a late lunch. Join us, please."

Eunice blushed. "That's a wonderful invitation, but I can't today. I've got too much to do. Josiah, you go on."

"There you have it. Permission to seek adventure granted by the beautiful Eunice. Now scoot and freshen up a bit. By the time I have had my lemonade, you can be ready."

As if pulled by an invisible hand, I rose from my chair and hurried to my bedroom to change. Baby met me at the door with a stern look of disapproval on his droopy face.

"I see Eunice put you in here," I said as I scratched behind his ears.

Baby shook his head as if to agree. Eunice was one human with whom Baby didn't argue. She was the alpha, and he knew it.

"Don't give me that look. I'm not letting you out to drool over Mr. McPherson's fine wool Savile Row suit. You'll stay in here until I leave and that's final."

Baby gave me a baleful look before he circled three times and lay on his faux fur bed.

Throwing off my work clothes, I took a quick shower and quickly dressed in an outfit that even Franklin would have approved. A dark blue cotton dress with a flared skirt, gold jewelry, white cashmere sweater, and dark flats. Simple, but elegant. Slapping on some lipstick and grabbing a light coat, I rushed down the hall to the

great room, and stopped just short at the end of the hall.
Taking a deep breath, I slowly sauntered into the room
where Teddy was quietly sipping his lemonade. I did my
best to assume an air of indifference.

He looked up and gave me the once-over.
Recognizing the designer of my dress, Teddy smiled and
the light from his excessively white teeth flooded the
room, blinding me.

His approval made me happy.

Oh dear. See why I'm cautious with this man!

Teddy is dangerous to my heart.

35

"So where did you two lovebirds go?" asked Franklin, lounging on my bed.

"It was just a casual date for a couple of hours," I insisted. "We drove around for awhile. Ate an early supper at a seafood restaurant by the river."

Baby jumped up on the bed, snuggling with Franklin.

"Baby!" I barked. "You know you're not supposed to be on my bed."

Franklin pulled Baby's massive head toward him and kissed the tip of the dog's nose. "Leave him alone. Who's a good boy, Baby?"

Baby arranged himself so his head was on Franklin's stomach as he stretched his entire two hundred pounds across the rest of the bed.

"There goes my mattress," I complained.

"Go on with the story," encouraged Franklin, rubbing Baby's ears while I pulled outfits from my closet for Franklin to approve or, as usual, not approve.

"That's it. We had a lovely time, and he drove me home."

"No smooching by the gentle, flowing waters of the Kentucky River?"

"Nothing like that. It was strictly G-rated."

"Sounds like a B rating, B standing for boring. Where are you going tonight?"

"Teddy wouldn't say. Just told me to wear a nice dress."

"That doesn't tell you much. Should it be a formal dress, cocktail dress, prom dress, church dress, business dress? It's too overwhelming to think about. Didn't you ask?'

"I was so stunned to get another invitation that I stammered okay and hung up."

Franklin sighed wearily. "We have been over and over this. You've got to play hard to get. No sophisticated man is going to fall head over heels for some middle-aged, dumpy hick who goes '*Un, duh, yeah, that's great. We be goin' to a barn dance?*'"

"I'm not as bad as that."

Franklin crossed his eyes, puckered his lips like a fish, and wiggled his ears.

Besides being astounded that Franklin could contort his face like that, I winced at the realization, "Oh dear. I do come across as some starry-eyed rube, don't I?" I flopped on the bed. "Maybe that's my charm. He's tired of jaded grand dames with legs up to their armpits. He wants someone simpler."

"Simple is what you are."

I scrunched my nose at him.

"Since you don't know where you're going, wear your black funeral dress with a strand of pearls, and put your hair in an old fashioned French Twist. Get out those black pumps. Of course you won't wear it as well as Audrey Hepburn, but you'll fit in anywhere with that '60s look."

"That could work," I admitted.

"Glad that's out of the way. Now we can talk about something that's been on my mind." Franklin pulled a small vial of pills from his pocket. "Would you care to explain this?"

I grabbed the vial out of Franklin's hand. "If you don't stay out of my stuff, so help me, I'm going to . . . I don't know what, but I'll do something." I was furious, but making a big deal out of it was not going to smooth over the situation.

Undeterred, Franklin said, "You can get mad all you want. You've been losing too much weight, but your face is puffy. It looks swollen, so I did a little detective work of my own and I found those." He pointed at the vial. "And what's more, I looked up what those pills are for." Franklin gave me a sympathetic look. "It's your kidneys, isn't it?"

I nodded. "Have you told anyone?"

"No. I wanted to talk to you first."

"Then don't. I haven't processed it yet myself. I need time."

"How bad is it?" asked Franklin as he gently placed a hand on my shoulder.

"Not that bad at the moment. Actually, I feel better than I have in a long time. I could go on for years without serious complications or tomorrow I might need a transplant. It's the roll of the dice." I grabbed Franklin's hand and squeezed. "Please keep this to yourself. All I want to do at the present is have fun. I don't want people to know."

Franklin squeezed back and smiled. "It will be our little secret." He jumped up and started rummaging through my closet. "Let's see if we can get those big tugboats of yours into these tiny little black shoes. Come on, girl. Get up. Mr. Right might be making his way here as we speak."

I stood up feeling like I had dodged a bullet. It wouldn't be the last time that I would feel that way during the next couple of weeks, but I had no way of knowing that while Franklin helped me get ready for my date.

I soon would though.

36

Our evening was a classic date. Teddy arrived promptly at the appointed time, opened the car door, and told me I looked stunning. Me–stunning?

We went to one of the area's best restaurants, where Teddy told funny stories, selected an appropriate wine, and paid for dinner. Then he brought me home, kissed me passionately at the door and, like the gentleman he was, watched until I was safely in my house before he drove off.

After that, we had breakfast several times at Keeneland's race course kitchen so Teddy could watch the horses train.

Was I falling in love? My feelings weren't as intense for Teddy as they had been for Jake, but I certainly was in "like."

That morning while I was stuffing biscuits and gravy in my mouth, Teddy watched in a curious, detached way.

"I have never understood the American custom of pouring grey slop with the consistency of tile grout over unleavened bread that should only be consumed as a last resort to avoid starving. Don't even get me started on grits or hominy."

"Hush up, boy. This is good eatin'." I thrust a fork of biscuit dripping with gravy at him. "Try it. You'll change your mind."

"Only if you point a gun at me," Teddy kidded.

"I could bring up the fine old English traditions of bubble and squeak, blood pudding, or smoked herring for breakfast. And don't get me started on bangers and mash. I mean, really."

"Try them. You'll change your mind."

"Only if you point a gun at me."

We both laughed.

Being with Teddy was easy, effortless, like floating down a calm, green river in an old inner tube on a sunny afternoon, while listening to birds sing on the riverbanks. I know that's a cliché, but there it is.

Only this is the South. Our rivers are home to water moccasins. You'd better watch out!

37

The phone rang.

Groggy, I looked at my radio clock. It was 2 am. Phone calls in the dead of night give me the chills. "Unknown" was listed on the caller ID screen. Maybe it was a wrong number. Against my better instincts, I answered,

"Hello?"

"Toots? Toots?"

"Walter?"

"I need help, Toots."

"Walter, the police are looking for you. They are going to arrest you for the murder of Emma Fisher."

"I heard."

"What makes the police think you killed Emma?"

"I went to see her at Bunny's apartment. We had a

heated argument. I guess the police found my fingerprints, and maybe have some witnesses who saw me leave, but I swear I didn't touch Emma Fisher. She was alive when I left."

"Why did you go see her?"

"Something didn't smell right to me. That dame knew more than she was telling. I was trying to make her spill, but she clammed up. I know she was lying. I'd bet my reputation on it."

"That's not saying much, Walter."

"Listen Toots, she had something to do with Bunny's death. I feel it in my bones. That's why I need to you do something for me."

"NO! You leave me out of this."

"You can't say no. I've got no one else to turn to. You've got to help me. You owe it to me."

I didn't respond because I didn't know what to say. It's true that I was responsible for foiling Walter's plan to steal a winning lottery ticket and then tased him to boot, but in my defense, he threatened an old woman, Ethel, and her cat, Petty, to get the ticket. Then he started working with Fred O'nan, my stalker, and was tailing me for that psycho, so what did I really owe Walter?

And considering our history, why was I feeling sorry for that loser?

"If you don't help me, I could be convicted on circumstantial evidence and spend the rest of my life in prison. You gotta help me. Please, Josiah. Please!"

"I don't know how I can be of any help, Walter."

"I would do it myself, but I can't leave the city. There's a BOLO out on me, and the police are watching all the car rentals, airports, and bus stations. Bunny's New York memorial is in three days. I want to you to go to it and talk to the cook–Theda Finkelstein."

"Whatever for?"

"I want you to ask her about Fisher's love life. I don't think she worked alone."

"Walter, that's just wishful thinking. Emma Fisher was a nice young woman who was in the wrong place at the wrong time."

"Don't be so naïve. Emma Fisher was from the wrong side of the tracks. She wanted money, and she didn't care how she got it, especially if she didn't have to work for it. Surely you must know the terms of the will by now."

"Emma had worked for Bunny for years. Bunny relied on her, said she was a devoted employee."

"How do you think the intruder was getting inside Bunny's apartments? Even you thought the front door didn't look like it had been forced, so the guy must have had a key and the codes to the security system. I know Bunny wouldn't give out the keys to her apartments. It had to be Emma, since Mrs. Finkelstein would not have access to the London or Lexington apartment keys."

"It could have been the building supers who were bribed to give out keys," I suggested.

Walter exclaimed, "In all the cities! Connect the dots, sweetheart. This broad was the link. She was in all the cities with Bunny–London, New York, and Lexington.

She had keys to all the homes, and she knew Bunny's schedule, plus all the security codes."

"What do you want me to find out from this cook?"

"Anything. Anything at all, but especially if Emma had met someone. If she was acting strangely. You know the drill."

"I'll go, Walter, but now you owe me one, buddy. You must never tell anyone you called me. I don't want Detective Goetz angry with me."

"Aw Toots, you're the best. Thank you. Thank you. Now one more thing. I put the keys to Bunny and Emma's New York apartments and the security codes in your mailbox. Check them out for me."

"I'm not going to ask how you obtained those, but how will I get in touch?"

My answer was the dial tone, which sounded like an angry honeybee buzzing, and buzzing, and buzzzzzzing.

38

Wearing a beige trench coat over my black funeral dress, matching leather gloves, oversized sunglasses, a big floppy hat, and a strand of pearls, I crept into the memorial service for Bunny Witt at the Church of St. Vincent Ferrer on Lexington Avenue.

I slid into a back pew and listened to various grand dames of Park Avenue spout platitudes about Bunny Witt of the Philadelphia Witts, not to be confused with the Boston Whitts. None of them sounded sincere, but appearances must be maintained. It wasn't long before everyone ran out of steam and the service ended. Mourners–and I'm using a little bit of latitude with that word–began drifting outside.

Several women and a few tottering old men went to speak with a woman entrenched on the front pew. Keeping an eye on the queue, I checked out the floral arrangements, even noting who had sent them and from which flower shop. You never know what detail might be important.

When the line had shrunk to several people, I got behind the last person and waited my turn. In a matter of a few minutes, I was face-to-face with an obviously traumatized, wizened old lady who looked to be in her late seventies or early eighties. She had been the only person in the vast cathedral to show genuine sorrow.

"Mrs. Finkelstein?"

The woman wiped her teary eyes with a crumpled handkerchief before focusing on me.

I felt like I was getting ready to kick a dog.

"Yes?"

"Mrs. Finkelstein, my name is Josiah Reynolds. I'm from Kentucky. I knew Mrs. Witt. She stayed with my friend, Lady Elsmere."

Mrs. Finkelstein's face lit up. "I know who you are, and you're an answer to my prayers. Please sit. I have so many questions to ask."

As I sat, Mrs. Finkelstein grabbed my hands in a firm grip and squeezed. "I keep calling a Detective Goetz, but he won't answer any of my questions." She looked at me for sympathy. "I just can't believe it. Both Bunny and Emma gone."

"It has been quite a shock to us in Kentucky as well."

"How could this have happened? I understand they have arrested a man for Emma's murder?"

"Oh? That must have been after I left Kentucky." I paused while processing the fact that Walter might have been arrested. I hope that twerp didn't squeal on me. I didn't want to be arrested for being an accessory after the fact.

I continued, "Mrs. Finkelstein, I have some questions I would like to ask you, too."

"Please, call me Theda. Finkelstein is such a mouthful."

I managed a tease of a smile. "Thank you. Please call me Josiah."

Theda nodded.

"Do you know who was arrested?" I asked. It could have been someone other than Walter.

"Some man Bunny hired to help find out who had been breaking into her apartments, but I don't see why he would murder Emma. It doesn't make sense unless he is insane."

Feeling that I had limited time with Theda, I went straight to my questions. "Bunny told me you had worked for her mother."

"She was a fine lady. Gracious. When she died, I stayed on, perhaps longer than I should have, but Bunny," Theda threw her hands up, "needed guidance. She was given to impulsive decisions. I did the best I could, but as you can see, it wasn't good enough."

"You don't need to take on such a burden, Theda. Lady Elsmere tried to reason with Bunny, but she was very headstrong."

"Is headstrong the word you would use?"

"I'm trying to be diplomatic."

Theda chuckled. "Damn stupid is what I would call her."

It was my turn to chuckle now. "But I understand she could be a great and generous friend. Emma told me how Bunny paid the medical bills when her father took ill."

Theda's brow furrowed. "What are you talking about? Emma's parents were dead by the time Emma started working for Bunny. They died in a boating accident while she was still in high school."

I tried not to look stunned. "I must have misunderstood." I hurried on to another question. "Had Emma worked for Bunny long?"

"Over ten years, I think. Maybe longer."

"Do you have any idea how someone could have gotten into the New York apartment without forcing the door?"

Theda looked down at her lap as she began smoothing out her dress.

"Theda?"

"I don't like to speak ill of the dead."

"Do you think Bunny was creating the illusion of a stalker to get attention?"

"Absolutely not. That was too imaginative for her. Bunny was strictly a literal person."

"Emma?"

Theda nodded slightly.

"What makes you think that?"

"Emma was a hardworking girl, very ambitious. I

don't think Bunny realized how much Emma did for her, nor did Bunny appreciate Emma. Emma might have grown to resent that."

"How do you mean?"

"Bunny was not a perceptive person. She simply couldn't conceive that Emma might envy the lifestyle Bunny was born into. I would watch Emma study Bunny. She seemed almost predatory. She copied how Bunny spoke, walked, her manner of dress, how she conducted herself. I warned Bunny, but she took my warning as a compliment. She thought it was cute."

"Did you feel Emma was up to mischief?"

"I felt she needed to see someone–a therapist. Emma was becoming too possessive. Perhaps obsessive might be a better word."

"You used the word becoming. What tipped Emma from simply emulating Bunny to something more serious?"

"It started about a year ago. I noticed a change in Emma. She was very excited about something, and I figured it must have been a man."

"Did she say she had a boyfriend?"

"No. Emma was very closed-mouthed about her personal life, but I did overhear her talking to someone on the telephone. When I walked into the room, she hung up abruptly. I asked her who it was, and she said it was a wrong number."

"So?"

"I listened to her conversation before I entered the

room, Josiah. She was speaking to a man. You know how the voice changes, special words that are spoken when talking to a new love, and I distinctly heard her agreeing to meet someone. Later, Emma became more secretive, and would be gone from the apartment for long periods of time, supposedly running errands, but I knew better. She would always come back looking a little disheveled."

"Like she had been enjoying a midday romp."

"Exactly."

"Did you ever see this man?"

Theda shook her head. "When I teased her about having a secret boyfriend, Emma would become defensive and deny it. I could tell she was lying. She wouldn't look at me."

"I met with Emma on the day she died. Among the many things she told me was that she was going to be in charge of Bunny's philanthropic foundation, and also receive the New York apartment with a maintenance stipend. How did that come about?"

"That nonsense arose a little after Emma started sneaking off. The will is almost the same. The main difference was that Emma was going to take over the charities. Initially it was to be the law firm that handled Bunny's affairs. They were the most qualified to handle all that money, in my opinion."

"That's one. Others?"

"All property, except for Ravensnest, was to be sold, and the money put in the philanthropic fund."

"What was to become of Ravensnest?"

"It was to go to a distant cousin."

"In other words, the farm was to stay in the family."

"Yes, that's correct. There was never a question about that."

"Emma told me Ravensnest was to be sold."

"Bunny would never have agreed for Ravensnest to be sold out of the family. Never."

"Who brought up making the changes? Bunny?"

"It was Emma. She kept badgering Bunny, saying that she was better equipped to handle the estate as the executrix since she knew all the details of Bunny's finances and property."

"She had a point there."

"Emma did, but it was not her place to say so. It was as if she was counting on Bunny dying. If the will needed to be upgraded, it should have been Bunny's idea–not Emma's. I thought the entire line of discussion unnecessary and morbid." Theda paused and looked at the memorial's oversized picture of Bunny strolling down Fifth Avenue in a Gucci outfit, looking young and vibrant.

"Who would have thought I would outlive my mistress' daughter and her young assistant," she whispered while wiping her moist eyes. "Life isn't fair, is it, Josiah?"

"No, ma'am. It sure as hell fire isn't."

A distinguished-looking man in his late fifties entered the church. He was wearing a navy double-breasted pinstripe suit with an orange patterned tie and matching handkerchief. Appearing overly dramatic by taking large, hurried steps, he came up to us, smiling.

Theda's face lit up when she saw him. "Josiah, this is my son, Harry . . ."

I held out my hand. "Harry Stein. I recognize you from your picture in the paper. I take it Stein is a stage name."

Harry shook it vigorously. "Finkelstein took up too much ink, and no one could pronounce it or spell it correctly, so I shortened it." He turned to his mother. "Sorry, Mom. My meeting took more time than I anticipated."

He addressed me as though he needed to explain his absence. "I was calming a leading lady who didn't like her dressing accommodations. It seemed the paint in her dressing room was not the correct shade of blue, and the toilet leaked." He raised his eyes as if to heaven. "That should be the extent of everyone's problems. Right? No illness. No money problems. No funerals. Just leaking commodes and bad paint jobs. Well, enough about me. Have you seen my current play?"

"Yes, during my last trip to New York. I enjoyed it very much."

Harry beamed. "Much gratified. Critics be damned, eh?"

Theda confessed, "I didn't want him to go into show business, but it's in our blood, I guess. My parents were a famous vaudevillian couple."

"Thus the name Theda, after Theda Bara, the silent screen actress," I guessed.

"She was a close friend of my mother's. I'm surprised you remember her."

"I've seen several of her films. She's hard to forget."

Theda put a finger up to her pursed lips and said, "That reminds me."

Harry asked, "What does, Mother?"

"I seem to recall that before Emma left for Kentucky, she was very agitated. When I asked what was wrong, she mumbled something about gaslight."

"Gaslight? Do you know what she meant?" I asked.

"When I pressed for more information, she cut me off, saying she needed to check something when she got to Lexington, but she wouldn't say what."

"And you have no idea what she was referring to?" I wanted to sit down with Theda and have a long talk, but knew my time was running out.

"None. I'm so sorry."

"Josiah, I'm sorry too," Harry said, "but we must take our leave of you. As you can see, this has been a considerable strain on Mother. I need to take her home to rest."

Jumping Jehosaphat! I needed more time. "Of course. Thank you for talking with me," I replied, wanting to appear sympathetic, but feeling quite put out. One does need to be polite under such circumstances. See? I'm not that bad.

Harry reached into his coat and took out his wallet. Handing a business card to me, he implored, "If you have any news about these dreadful murders, please call me at the number on the card. We would be most grateful to be kept updated on the progress of the investigation."

Theda nodded. "Yes, please keep us informed."

Taking the card, I slipped it into my purse. "I will do my best," I promised. After saying my thank-you's, I headed back to Asa's apartment, my home away from home in the Big Apple.

39

Feeling surprisingly strong with energy to spare, I directed the cab driver to the Dakota instead of my daughter's apartment, but the traffic was so horrible that by the time we arrived, my energy had been sapped. Well, I was here now. Might as well get out.

I paid the cab driver and wondered how I could waltz past the doorman. The last time I had been with Bunny, so it had been no problem. I remembered that Bunny had called him Bob. I decided on the tactic of bravado.

Walking past Bob with an imperial air, I inclined my head just a little and said, "Good afternoon, Bob."

"Good afternoon, ma'am," replied Bob, tipping his hat. Puzzled, he glanced down at his clipboard and then at me, but all he could see was my back. I was hightailing it to the elevators.

So far, so good.

I pushed the buttons for three different floors in case Bob decided to rush after me and check my ID. It would take him a while to locate me after the elevator doors had closed. Getting out on Bunny's floor, I hurried to her door and let myself in, glad no one had seen me. Checking the security system, I saw that it was disarmed.

I flipped the light switch and the lamps came on. Good! The electricity was still on.

The apartment was musty, not having been used in over a month. There was a faint layer of dust on the furniture. Quickly looking around, I discovered there was no mail and no newspapers. The building super must be collecting for Bunny. Nothing I could do about that.

Now to search, but where should I start? Where do people hide things?

I went into the kitchen first. Knowing Bunny, hidden items would be where she could find them readily. I checked the freezer. Nothing concealed with the brisket or lamb. Checked all the dry goods canisters, dipping my hand in the flour and sugar containers. Nada. Looked under the breakfast table. Clean.

Now moving to her office. Sitting at Bunny's desk, I shuffled through her papers. Nothing exciting. Coming across an address book, I shoved it into my bag. I imagined it must be her mother's. Most people put phone numbers and addresses on their cell phone these days. Only dinosaurs like me still have an old-fashioned address book. I would read it later. Who knows? Might have a contact in it that would solve her murder.

I continued my search by checking behind paintings, opening the backs of frames that held family photographs. Bunny said she had had a safe, but where was it? This search was getting boring.

Yawning, I made my way to the master suite. Starting with the bathroom, I checked inside the toilet tank. Just blue water. Checked the medicine cabinet, the linen closet, even the inside of toilet paper rolls. A total blank.

With what little energy I had left, I pulled out the drawers from her dressers, checking underneath and behind them.

Felt underneath the mattress. Having no luck there, I finally faced her walk-in closet. This would take some time.

I went through every piece of clothing, checked every pocket, felt every lining, looked through every shoe, hat, glove, purse, piece of luggage until I was utterly spent. I tapped the walls for hidden safes. Still, I couldn't find the safe. Didn't Bunny say she had a safe? Finally, I gave up the ghost.

If there was something here that would shine light on Bunny's death, I couldn't find it.

Exhausted and having difficulty breathing, I fled the apartment, going by the way of the service elevator. A half a block away, I hailed a cab and gave the address to Asa's apartment. It was dark now, and I needed some serious rest.

Emma's apartment would have to wait.

40

I had four hours before my plane left for Lexington. That should be enough time to check Emma's apartment before heading out to the airport.

The cab driver stopped in front of Emma's building in Greenwich Village. I promised him a hundred-dollar tip plus fare if he waited for me. I thought it was fair since he was also keeping an eye on my luggage, and I had no idea how long he would have to wait for me.

Emma's apartment was on the fourth floor of a five-floor walk-up. Great. It took fifteen minutes to climb those stairs. By the time I reached her door, I was sweating so profusely, my makeup was slipping down my face and onto my clothes. I didn't even want to imagine what a fright I looked.

I unlocked the front door and slowly opened it, peeking inside. I don't know what I expected. It just pays to be careful.

Sometimes a little paranoia comes in handy. You caught me. I will admit I'm paranoid. Wouldn't you be, if you were me?

Again, there was no sign that the police had visited, which I thought odd. There was no crime scene tape sealing the front, nor any visible signs of dusting for prints inside. It had been the same at Bunny's apartment.

Perhaps the police hadn't gotten to the apartments yet because they were snowed under with New York murders. Anyway, that was all the better for me, but I still made sure I had on gloves. I was taking a big risk. It could be interpreted that I was tampering with evidence if I had the misfortune to be nabbed by New York's finest.

Emma's apartment was a small, one-bedroom affair. Unlike Bunny, who had expensive, prestigious beige furniture, Emma was an Ikea gal and liked color–big blocks of bold, fun color. I could say that I preferred Emma's apartment. It was light and airy as much as it was exuberant–the kind of exuberance that comes with being young and believing everything is possible.

Looking around at the cheerful apartment, I felt a little sad. Emma had been hopeful about something. What was it? Was it because Emma knew she was going to inherit a lot of money because she had planned Bunny's death? Or was it that she had met someone and was in love?

I hoped it was the latter. Maybe I could find the answer by searching. I hurried after looking at my watch.

I was running out of time. No way was I going to miss my flight.

I did my regular routine of snooping and found nothing. Finally, I was in her clothes closet. I rushed through Emma's clothes, praying that my cab was still outside. Nothing. I pushed them aside and tapped the walls. Sounded solid. Frustrated, looking around the closet, I was flummoxed about what to do next. It was then I noticed the left rear corner of the carpet was pulled up just a tad–barely noticeable. Some of the backing threads were visible. Hmm?

Using my cane, I hooked the wolf's snout on the tab of carpet and pulled back. A manila mailing envelope peeked out. Grasping a chair, I sat down and carefully leaned over, grabbing the carpet and pulling with all my might. The carpet gave way, exposing several large first-class mailers. Eureka!

Well, well, well. It seemed our little Emma was a glass full of sass, after all.

41

I had used my cell phone to photograph the documents I discovered in Emma's apartment. Once back home, I laid the photographs out on my Nakashima table. I spent hours studying them.

Jumping Jehosaphat! These babies were dynamite.

They were copies of Bunny's insurance inventories of her jewelry, art work, and couture dresses. Also included were hand-drawn floor plans of the apartments in London, New York, and Lexington. Between the sheets of paper in the manila envelopes was a napkin from the Rose Bar in the Gramercy Park Hotel with numbers hastily written on it with what I presumed to be lipstick. I assumed the numbers to be the combination to a safe.

But here's the rub. Why would Emma compile and hide these documents? She already knew the floor plans of the apartments, and had access to Bunny's insurance lists any time she wanted. All she had to do was open a file drawer or a computer file to review the information.

It was as if she was amassing the information for someone else, but why didn't that person have the manila envelope in their possession?

Why was Emma hiding it?

Because Emma was storing the information for him, her, or them. Someone wanted access to the information anytime they needed it, but didn't want to be caught with the information in their home, computer, or on his/her person. That meant they had access to Emma anytime they wanted.

So Theda was right.

Emma was seeing someone, and this person didn't want Emma to share that information with even her closest associates.

Why did I believe that?

Think, darling, think. I found no pictures, love letters, trinkets a lover would get for another in newfound love.

Emma's apartment looked like a bachelor lady's with no family or love interests living there. It was barren of all the bits and pieces of paper, photographs, toys, and mementoes that connect us to others.

Emma must have been a very lonely person. She was ripe for the picking by some manipulative person.

Somehow Emma must have come to the realization that she had been used.

No wonder she had been terrified.

42

I was at the Farmers' Market on a Saturday morning selling my honey. Business had been brisk that cool morning, but I was currently experiencing a lull. It was fine by me when Shaneika dropped off her son, Lincoln Warfield Todd, while she shopped.

Linc was a born businessman and loved to take over my kiosk when he visited. He was never flustered by multiple purchases or demanding customers, and he could count change back the old-fashioned way–using his noggin.

Giving Linc free rein of my portable shop, I sat in my lounge chair sipping hot chocolate, happily content–until I felt a hand on my shoulder.

Not liking people coming up behind me, I naturally flinched and automatically reached in my pocket for my Taser.

"Josiah."

I turned in my chair. "Holy Moly! I wish you wouldn't sneak up behind me, Goetz. I don't like it."

Goetz' expression immediately let me know this was not a social visit. He had on his "detective" face.

"Josiah, I need you to come with me."

"Where to?"

"To the station. This is official business."

I rose from my chair. "Why?" I have a naturally defiant reaction to authority.

"I need to ask you some questions."

"You know I can refuse to talk to you."

"Then I'll just have to arrest you right here at the Farmer's Market in front of everyone."

My stomach tightened. "On what charge?"

"Tampering with evidence and obstruction of justice for starters."

Goetz got out his handcuffs.

"Put those away," I hissed. "I'll come. Don't embarrass me."

With a smug grin, Goetz put them away.

I removed the straw hat and apron I usually wore at the Market and turned my back to Goetz. I could tell my face was flushed, and I didn't want Goetz to see how flustered I was. "Lincoln, will you watch my things until your Mama comes back?"

Lincoln nodded, his wide eyes never leaving Goetz.

"Will you tell her that I'm with Detective Goetz, and she is to come to the police station for me?"

"Yes."

"I'll call Matt to come and pack up my things."

"I'll watch till he comes."

Smiling, I softly touched Linc's velvet cheek. "I know you'll do me proud. Remember to tell your mother where I am, and that she's to come for me."

"Yes, ma'am."

I followed Goetz to a police vehicle and got in the back. The weasel wouldn't let me ride shotgun. I felt totally humiliated, aware that all eyes were upon me. At that moment, I really hated him.

‘

43

If Goetz wanted to play hardball, so could I.

I refused to speak until Shaneika arrived and I had time to converse with her.

Three and a half hours later, I was sitting in an interrogation room with Shaneika by my side and Goetz sitting across a battered table. It was the same room and across the same nasty table where I had been interrogated about the death of Richard Pidgeon only a few short years ago. Only it had been Fred O'nan who interrogated me with Goetz passively standing by. He wasn't passive today.

I involuntarily shivered from fear.

"Are you cold?" asked Shaneika.

I shook my head.

Shaneika turned to Goetz. "What's this about, Detective?"

"Shaking the tree to see what falls to the ground."

"You damaged my client's reputation by making a scene at her place of work."

Goetz grinned. "Ms. Todd, you know next week Josiah's booth will be bombarded with curious folks wanting to get the lowdown on what happened today."

He looked at me and winked. "You better bring more honey next week. You'll probably sell out."

I wanted to reach across the table and slap Goetz' smug face, but I sat still. Sometimes I actually exercise impulse control.

"Is my client under arrest?" Shaneika demanded.

Mugging, Goetz answered, "Depends on what your client tells me."

"About what?" I interjected.

"Tampering with evidence concerning Emma Fisher's death."

"I haven't tampered with anything."

Goetz took a picture from a folder and threw it across the table. "Do you deny this is you entering Emma Fisher's apartment in New York?"

Jumping Jehosaphat! Play it cool, girl. Play it cool.

I made a big production of reaching into my purse and retrieving a pair of reading glasses. I put them on and leaned over the photograph. "Yeah, that's me. So what?"

"So you admit it's you."

"I just said so."

"Then you admit you broke into Emma Fisher's apartment after her death."

"I admit no such thing. I admit I entered her apartment, but I didn't break into it. As it so happens, I had a key."

"How did you happen to have Emma's apartment key?"

"Emma gave it to me the day we met at the Chevy Chase Inn," I lied. "Do you have a picture in your little folder of me sitting in a booth knocking back a Bloody Mary that day? It seems you've been keeping tabs on me."

"This is nothing more that police harassment," concurred Shaneika.

Goetz leaned back in his chair. He pursed his lips ever so slightly.

I could tell he didn't expect me to have a key. Goetz didn't like having the wind taken out of his sails.

"And there was no reason for me not to enter the apartment, since there was no crime scene tape nor a post telling anyone they couldn't enter the apartment," I continued.

"Why were you there?"

"Emma was worried. She told me if something happened to her, I was to water her plants."

Goetz closed his eyes, slowly inhaled deeply, holding his breath for a few seconds and exhaled. He opened his eyes. "You know being a smart-ass is not going to help you here," he shot back.

"I guess not, but it makes me feel a whole better."

"Josiah," cautioned Shaneika, "let me handle this."

Goetz took out another photograph of me handling the manila envelopes I found in Emma's closet. "Care to explain this? You went right to them. How did you know they were hidden in the closet?"

"I didn't. I looked in the closet and saw fibers sticking up from the corner of the carpet and pulled them up. That's how I found the envelopes. I didn't know they were there."

"The New York boys had already found the envelopes. They set up a motion-activated camera in the apartment, wanting to see who paid a visit, and if they would go to the closet—and in you stumble, as big as life." He threw out some more pictures of me searching the apartment.

"So I found some large envelopes in the apartment, but I didn't leave with them. I took pictures of the contents and then put the envelopes back where I found them. I didn't tamper with anything. I didn't even leave my fingerprints on them. This so-called evidence is pristine."

"Why were you there?"

"I told you—to water Emma's plants."

"She didn't have any plants."

"I must have misunderstood."

Shaneika pointed out, "Detective Goetz, no crime has been committed here. Mrs. Reynolds did not break into the apartment. She had a key. There was no posting by the New York police that she couldn't enter.

"Fact number two–she didn't remove anything from the apartment, or take any of the contents, including the envelopes from the closet, which she put back. All she did was take photographs of the material inside. Now you may construe this to be tampering with evidence, but it would very hard to get a jury to agree with you, considering the injustices that Mrs. Reynolds has had to endure from the hands of the police."

Goetz stiffened. "Who gave you that key?"

"I told you–Emma Fisher. Since we're discussing the murder of Emma Fisher–how did she die?" I asked.

"She was strangled with a scarf."

I curled my lip. "That takes a lot of strength and anger. I can't believe you think Walter did it. He wasn't as tall as Emma."

"It doesn't take much height to strangle a woman with her own scarf when she's sitting and come up from behind."

"Oh," I blurted. "And you found Walter's DNA on the scarf?"

Goetz looked at his wristwatch. "Time is 3:45 pm, and this interview is concluded." Once he had turned the video camera off, Goetz announced, "We had to let Walter Neff go, but he's still a suspect."

"That means you couldn't tie him to the murder, or Walter had a solid alibi for the time of Emma's death. What about Bunny?" I asked.

"That's all I can tell you. Both murders are still under investigation."

Shaneika stood up. "Come on, Josiah. Let's go before we waste more of Detective Goetz' time or you say something stupid."

Say something stupid? Who, me?

44

Later that same day, I hurried to the boat dock where June and I kept our boats on the Kentucky River. Snatching the key out of a hole in a sycamore tree, I started June's pontoon boat and headed down the river to the public boat ramp where I had arranged to meet Walter Neff.

Thirty minutes later, I pulled the pontoon over to the riverbank and Walter jumped in. We then sped further down the river.

Walter slumped down in a seat next to the captain's chair and wiped his sweaty face off with an old towel left on the boat. "This is very cloak and dagger, even for you, Toots."

"I want to make sure that we're not followed. I have spent the day being grilled by the police, and I don't want to give them any reason to take another shot at me." I handed him the photos of the documents from Emma's apartment.

Pulling over around a bend in the river, I tied the boat to an overhanging branch, making sure no snakes were sunning on it first. Relaxing in the captain's chair, I watched Walter peruse the pictures. "What do you think?"

Walter laid them out on the small table before him. "These make it look like Emma was planning to kill Bunny."

"I disagree. Why would she need to make drawings of the floor plans and a listing of the security codes? That makes no sense. It looks to me like she was cataloguing this information for someone else. Theda Finkelstein was positive Emma was secretly seeing someone."

"Yeah, but who, Toots? I need something other than an old lady's instinct. I need something I can sink my teeth into. I need proof. My neck is in the noose as we speak."

"Mrs. Finkelstein didn't know whom she was seeing."

"Hunky-dory that's not. Gets me nowhere."

"It gets you everywhere, Walter. There's someone in the background controlling the lives of these two women."

"And he used Emma to kill my baby."

"Are you accusing Emma of killing Bunny? I didn't even see her at the gala."

"She could have snuck in."

"There was security at the gate and all guests had to have an invitation. The thing to check is whether Emma's name was on the guest list, and if she was checked off by security."

"How would I do that?"

"You're a private investigator, so investigate."

"Let's go over why Emma wanted to see you."

"I have never figured out why Emma wanted to see me. I was not close to Bunny, and didn't know Emma at all."

"But Emma said she was frightened?"

"Yes, and I have no idea what she wanted me to do about it. The meeting with her is still a mystery to me."

"Didn't she say something to Mrs. Finkelstein about being frightened, too?"

"She told Mrs. Finkelstein something about gaslight."

"Gaslight? What the heck is that about?"

"Walter, I've helped you all I can. I've put myself at risk meeting with you. Now I'm done. I'm going to drop you off at the dock and we're finished. Capisce?"

"You copping out on me, Toots?"

"Walter, I'm tired, and I don't feel well today. Bunny was neither my client nor my friend. The ball is in your court. Run with it."

"I liked Bunny Witt. I thought we hit if off real good–like there might be a future there, you know? So why was she sneaking off to meet someone at the gala?"

"You don't know that, Walter. She could have been lured with a note from a friend, or a potential buyer saying they wanted a private talk about buying her dresses. You don't know that Bunny going out to the carriage house had anything to do with a lovers' rendezvous."

I turned the pontoon boat around and headed back to the public dock while Walter continued to argue with me.

I was abandoning him in his hour of need. How could I be so heartless? I had access to information he didn't have. He was depressed and needed someone to talk with. Yada. Yada. Yada.

"For goodness' sake, Walter! Take your marbles and find someone else to play with."

45

The fruit trees, apples, pears, and peaches were in bloom and alive with the sound of bees happily pollinating as they gathered nectar.

The nectar mixes with chemicals in the bees' stomachs, and is taken back to the hive where it is stored in hexagonally-shaped wax cells. The house bees then flap their wings to help evaporate water from the nectar. Once that is accomplished, the cell is sealed with more wax and left for food use down the road. Once enough cells are covered with wax, I harvest the honey.

Don't worry. I leave enough honey for the bees, which make approximately five hundred pounds a year per hive. I only take a hundred pounds or so.

That's a lot to keep up with, and soon the days ran into each other. I pushed the deaths of Bunny Witt and Emma Fisher to the back of my mind. I had bees to manage, horses to board, animals to feed, doctor appointments to keep, and a business with Eunice to run. I was quite the busy gal.

Oh, did I tell you that Teddy and I were seeing quite a bit of each other? We were social gadabouts, going to parties, receptions, charity balls, dinner parties–you know–the usual social functions with Lexington's upper elite. When not glad-handing, we went to the movies or out to dinner. I'm sure all this running around was not good for my health, but I didn't care. I was having fun.

Teddy was sophisticated, fun, witty, and charming. He was always well dressed, smelled divine, and his manners were impeccable. Oh, did I mention handsome? In other words, he was a catch.

So what was the problem, you may wonder? Who says there's a problem?

I do, that's who. Besides throwing caution to the wind about my health, what the hell was Teddy doing with me? He could have had any available gal in Lexington, so why was he hand-holding with me?

Am I paranoid? No. Just the facts, ma'am. And the facts were this–I wasn't good enough. I'm not talking about personal worth. I'm talking about looks and money. This guy was slick, looked like a movie star, and behaved with aplomb.

Usually I was lucky to remember to brush my hair before I left the Butterfly, though I did make an effort to look well-groomed for Teddy, but there was only so much I could do. Let's face it. I definitely had peaked some years back.

So again, I ask you. What was Teddy McPherson doing with me?

And it worried me.

We had been invited to Lady Elsmere's house for tea at four.

Usually I just barge through the kitchen door, but on this occasion we knocked formally on the front door. I could see Teddy was impressed with the enormous portico that graced the front of the Big House.

"My late husband restored this treasure after Lady Elsmere came back to America and bought the farm," I told him.

"He did a wonderful job," agreed Teddy. "As Queen Elizabeth I said when she learned her sister, Queen Mary had died, 'It is marvelous in our eyes.'"

"Yes. 'This is the Lord's doing, and it is marvelous in our eyes.' She was quoting from the Bible."

"Was she?" replied Teddy, swiveling toward the door as it opened. "That's the only thing I remember from school besides the fabulous jewels she wore in her official portraits. Such clarity of color. Such brilliance."

"Hello, Charles," I said. "We've come to tea."

Charles, dressed in his formal attire, took our wraps and gloves.

While I was handing Charles my coat, I couldn't help but think that Teddy's remarks were odd, but I pushed them from my mind, as I usually do when things don't fit, and let Charles escort us to the library.

Lady Elsmere was waiting, dressed in a dark green taffeta and silk dress accentuated by her splendid emerald and diamond earrings and necklace, looking very regal.

"My dear lady. Thank you for inviting us for tea and sharing your magnificent home," remarked Teddy, bending over to kiss June's hand.

I thought Teddy was a little over the top, but June was eating up his words and demeanor like candy.

As Teddy sat next to June on the couch, I plopped in a chair by the fire. That way I could get a good view of them complimenting each other. I thought I was going to lapse into a diabetic coma from the syrupy words spilling from their mouths, but I resigned myself to the lovefest. Teddy adored beautiful things, and my friend June, Lady Elsmere, owned a multitude of beautiful things. They had a great deal in common.

"Josiah tells me you were born in London?" asked June, trying to lift the teapot.

"Here, let me help you. That looks too heavy," offered Teddy, grabbing the sterling silver teapot. "Milk? Sugar?" he asked while pouring.

Liam entered with several trays of finger sandwiches and tiny cakes.

"I'll have mine plain, please," I remarked, catching Liam's eye and giving an almost imperceptible nod.

He set the trays down and left. Neither he nor June acknowledged one another. I guess Liam was still in the doghouse.

Speaking of dogs, I heard Ginger barking upstairs. She must know tea was being served, and wanted Matt to attend. Whenever Matt was present for tea, Ginger would beg a treat or two from him.

"You said you were born in London," repeated June, "but your name is Scottish."

"Right you are, My Lady," concurred Teddy. "My mother was English, and my father was Scottish. He was in the Navy, and was on leave when he met my mother. They quickly fell in love and thus—here I am."

June clapped her hands in merriment. "A delightful anecdote. How did you reach our fair shores, Mr. McPherson?"

"Teddy, please. May I be so bold as to call you June?"

"I'd be crushed if you didn't."

"My job is simple, Lady Elsmere . . . I mean June. I'm in the business of procuring things, usually items of great beauty and worth."

"What does that mean exactly, Teddy?" asked June.

"I arrange things. People come to me with a request, and I try to fulfill the demand."

I took a sip of my tea and then inquired, "Such as arranging the couture exhibit?"

Teddy looked at me with a ghost of a smile. "Exactly."

"And who is the benefactor of this exhibit?" asked June, looking innocent.

"The sponsor would like to remain anonymous," replied Teddy. "This reminds me of an old Zulu tactic called the Water Buffalo. The two horns of the Water

Buffalo go left and right until they circle the enemy and
catch him within their grasp." Teddy glanced back and
forth from me to June as he made this last remark.

June's eyes narrowed as she fingered her emerald
necklace. "I hope you're not suggesting that Josiah and I
resemble buffalos."

"No, dear lady, I was referring to you and Josiah
maneuvering to get information out of me using
something like the Zulu Water Buffalo technique," Teddy
laughed. "I would like to get information out of you, too.
June, where did you acquired that stunning necklace?
The large emerald in the center is the Kaur emerald, is it
not?"

June showed surprise. Not many people knew she
owned the Kaur emerald.

"You certainly know your gems, Teddy. I wore the
necklace in your honor."

The talk of gems stopped when Matt and Franklin
jaunted into the library, "May we join you?"

I noticed Teddy's eyes move swiftly across Matt as if
sizing him up. I couldn't fault him. Matt, though
ravaged, was still hauntingly stunning.

Matt reached over and shook Teddy's hand. "Franklin
and I were at the gala, but we didn't have the opportunity
to converse with you. It was a well-done affair. Very
impressive."

Teddy smiled. "Thank you. I appreciate the
feedback."

"Teddy, this is Matthew and Franklin. Matthew is staying with me while he renovates his bungalow on Josiah's property," introduced June.

"Where is that?" asked Teddy, reaching over and shaking Franklin's hand.

I offered, "It's the little shack on the left as you come up my driveway."

"Oh, that building. It's hardly a shack," mused Teddy, grinning.

"Believe me, before it was restored, it was definitely a shack that even the crows wouldn't light on," stated Franklin before taking a bite out of a scone. "Is there any more tea?"

Teddy reached for the teapot. "Sorry, old man. Let me pour you a cup."

"It used to be the caretaker's house," I said, remembering more lucrative times, when Brannon and I had first built the Butterfly.

"Milk?" asked Teddy before pouring tea for Franklin.

I noticed that Teddy poured the milk in first for Franklin's tea, which was an insult in upper class English circles. Historically, only the lower classes put in milk first, because they used inferior dishware. Pouring hot tea first risked cracking the cup. Only the upper classes put tea in first, for they used porcelain.

I pursed my lips tightly, but said nothing.

"Matt, I understand you have a new baby," Teddy bantered, handing a cup of tea to Franklin.

"Yes, that's right. She's the apple of my eye."

Franklin rolled his eyes. "Since that baby was born, everything Matt does or says is a cliché from the fifties. Apple of his eye. She's more a little demon."

"Oh, like you don't worship her," Matt shot back.

"What's the baby's name?" asked Teddy.

"Emmeline Louise Rose Garth. Those are the middle names of my mother, Rennie, and Lady Elsmere," announced Matt proudly, looking at June and me.

"Who is Rennie?"

"Me," I chirped. "That's Matt's pet name for me, after the actor Michael Rennie. We met at a party, and I helped Matt settle a bet about what Michael Rennie's character said to Gort, the robot, in *The Day The Earth Stood Still.*"

"Klaatu barada nikto," recited Teddy. "But wasn't it Patricia Neal who said that to Gort?"

Franklin clapped his hands in glee. "Gotcha on that one, Josiah."

"I won a lot of money with that bet, so I call Josiah Rennie," Matt said.

Teddy said, "Josiah, you didn't tell me there was another man in your life."

"I'm just a good friend," assured Matt, looking between Teddy and me.

Franklin snorted.

June came to the rescue. "I believe I hear the little demon crying."

Franklin rushed to the door and opened it, which

allowed Ginger, who had been waiting to receive her treat, dash in. She took several tentative steps into the room before stopping and sniffing the air. Suddenly Ginger's hackles rose and a low growl sounded from deep in her chest.

Matt snapped to attention. "Ginger? What's wrong, girl?" He turned to us. "I'm so sorry. She's never done this before." Tugging on her collar, Matt pulled Ginger out of the room while chastising her. "Bad doggie. BAD!"

Teddy stood abruptly. "Lady Elsmere . . . I mean June. This has been a delightful afternoon, but Josiah and I have an early dinner reservation. Josiah," he said, extending his hand to me.

Looking confused, June declared, "I'm so sorry. Ginger has never acted like that before. Perhaps she has an upset stomach."

"I'm sure that's it. Something in the room excited her. Perhaps because the tea was Oolong instead of Earl Grey," I remarked.

June lifted her cheek to receive my kiss. "Earl Grey is a morning tea." She paused for a moment before remembering, "You're still coming to my birthday party, aren't you? It's next week. Have you RSVP'd? We must have a head count for the caterer."

Teddy bent down and kissed June's hand. "We wouldn't miss it for the world, would we, Josiah?"

"I wouldn't miss it," I replied, emphasizing the word I. Teddy was a bit presumptuous to assume that he would be escorting me. For some reason it irritated me. Perhaps Ginger's growling had unnerved me.

Teddy gave me a curious look before shining his choppers at me.

On this occasion the blinding light from his teeth did not dispel the damp in the room.

Curious.

46

"My emerald necklace is gone!" accused June. "You stole it."

"I did not. It wasn't me," Liam rebutted.

"Who else knew where I kept it? It had to be you. Josiah gets you out of jail. I welcome you back into my household, and this is how you repay me!"

"My Lady, there were over a hundred people in the house last night, and they had the run of the place. It could have been anyone," Liam fired back.

I marched in where angels feared to tread—never come between a woman and her jewelry . . . or chocolate. Being in June's line of fire was definitely hazardous to one's health. She had the power, the money, and the connections to make one's life miserable if she so chose. "June, you were taking people up to your bedroom to see your jewelry collection. Did you lock the safe every time you went back downstairs?"

June looked puzzled. "I don't remember. I'm sure I did."

"But you don't remember, do you?" I said gently. I could tell June was distressed. "Charles, was anyone standing guard in June's room?"

"The upstairs had been roped off. No one was supposed to be up there except Emmeline and the sitter. Matt was downstairs helping me." Charles gave a remorseful stare at June. "You've been very naughty, Lady Elsmere. We talked about security before the party. No one was supposed to go upstairs."

"What's the point of having beautiful things if you can't show them?" complained June.

Matt added, "When I saw the elevator go up, I knew people were using it, so I went upstairs and escorted everyone down. That was about nine. I switched off the elevator and gave the key to Charles."

"I went straight to Her Ladyship's room, locked the safe, and then locked the closet door to the safe. After that, I locked all the bedroom doors," affirmed Charles.

"Did you check the rooms first?" I asked.

Charles shook his head. "Didn't have time. Too much going on. I needed to check to make sure the birthday cake had been assembled and would be ready at 9:30."

"The party started at eight, so that gave anyone an hour to steal your jewelry," I wondered out loud. "June, do you remember who was in your bedroom?"

"I don't need to remember. Liam stole my necklace. It's an heirloom. When I die, it's supposed to go back to the current Lord Elsmere. I have to find that necklace. Liam, give it to me."

I could see that June was going to be stubborn, more so out of fear than actually believing Liam had stolen the emerald and diamond necklace. She hadn't remembered the security protocols she was to have followed, nor the guests she had invited to see her gem collection. June was slipping, and she knew it.

I expressed the obvious as softly as I could. "Liam couldn't possibly have stolen the necklace, dear. He was helping the caterer in the kitchen all evening. The caterer has already vouched for Liam. His alibi is tight."

"Then he had an accomplice," insisted June. "Liam took my necklace. I know he did."

"Let's do this," suggested Matt. "Amelia, Franklin, and I will do a top-to-bottom search of the house. If we can't find it, I'll call the police. We'll need a report for the insurance company. It was insured, wasn't it?"

Charles nodded while June wailed, "This isn't about the money. The late Lord Elsmere entrusted the necklace to me. I am to return it. I must keep faith with his family. Oh, Liam, please tell me what you did with it."

Liam looked helplessly at June, not knowing what to do or say to comfort her. He hung his head and murmured, "I didn't take it, June. I swear it."

"Liam, pack your things," I advised. "You'll be staying with me until this is resolved. You can help

Eunice. I understand she's rented my house out for a wedding reception this Saturday."

Liam gave June one last pitiful look before he trudged out of the parlor.

I had a glimmer of recognition that Liam might actually care for June. Oh, he wasn't in love with her. Romantic love was out of the question, even though those two has trysted a time or two. I think he cared for June, the actual person who was June Webster, out of Monkey's Eyebrow, Kentucky–not the glamour, the money, or the British title. Liam wanted June to think well of him. He might be faking his concern for her as Charles believed, but I didn't think so.

It's so hard to ascertain another person's true intention.

Just consider my experience with my late husband, Brannon.

Look at me with Jake.

Look at me with Goetz.

On second thought, don't look. It's a mess.

47

Looking through my desk drawers for some legal pads, I came across Bunny's address book and her aunt's diary. Golly, I forgot to give them back. And to make matters worse, the diary was damaged from when I had left it outside in the dew.

I thumbed through the diary, wondering if it could be restored when I noticed the front end page was separating from inside the cover. While wondering if I could fix the beautiful red marbled end page with Elmer's glue, I was fiddling with it when I felt something underneath. Peeking between the end page and the cover I could just make out some writing.

My heart raced.

Hurrying into my bathroom with the diary, I gathered my eyebrow tweezers. After using my arm to swipe everything off my dressing table, I set the book under the magnifying makeup light. I would clean up the mess later. Carefully, I peeled the rest of the end page from the back of the front cover. It came undone readily.

Holding my breath, I slowly extracted two pieces of yellowing paper from their hiding place and carefully laid them on my table.

They were handwritten receipts which had addresses with dates. 1954! London!

One was from a London dressmaker for making a strapless white satin evening dress.

I thought that odd. That style would have been an inappropriate evening dress for Bunny's great aunt in 1954. She would have been far too old to wear a dress like that, and usually older women like to cover their arms and back. At least, that was my opinion.

The other receipt was for a large, jeweled clip from a London jeweler.

I went into the office holding the receipt and looked up the business on my computer. I couldn't find anything.

Hmm. Who was old and had lived in London that I knew? Picking up the phone, I dialed June's private line. "Hello, June? June, be quiet and listen to me. You can rake me over the coals later. Have you ever heard of a London jeweler by the name of Mr. Antony? Say around 1954. Unhuh. Unhuh. Oh, really? It did! You're sure it went out of business in the '70s. You're sure, now? Thanks, doll. Talk to you later."

If I could whistle, I would have whistled—for I believed I knew where the missing gems were stashed.

48

"Hello. Mr. Finkelstein. This is Josiah Reynolds. We met at Bunny Witt's memorial. Yes. Thank you. I'm fine. Okay, Harry it is. Harry, I need to speak with your mother. Is she with you? Thank you. Hello? Theda? I'm fine, thank you. I need to ask you a question about Emma. Yes, that's right. You told me she said something to you about gaslight. I need to know the exact context of Emma's use of the word. Was she looking for a gas stove or an old-fashioned gaslight for decoration? Unhuh. Unhuh. That's exactly how she used the word? Emma said she was 'being gaslighted?'

"Does it mean anything? I think it means everything. You've been most helpful. I think it explains why Emma was murdered. Do I know who? I think I do. I don't want to say a name until I'm sure. Yes, I'll be safe. I'll keep in touch, I promise. Gotta go now. Good-bye."

49

I kept a lookout while Liam took out his professional lock picking kit and, after working for only a few minutes, unlocked the back wrought iron gate to Hilltop Manor.

Taking the lead, Liam crept silently while I followed, trying not to bump into the outdoor furniture and bushes. All the lights in the mansion were out, and there were no cars in the parking lot. So far, so good.

With just a few clicks, Liam unlocked the back door. We crept inside.

Turning on my flashlight, we cautiously made our way to the main exhibit hall, and still, I ran right into a wall. "Shhhh," I shushed to no one in particular.

"What are we looking for?" asked Liam.

"A white dress with some sort of jeweled clasp or sash," I whispered.

"I don't know why we're being so quiet. No one is here," complained Liam.

I motioned for Liam to search one side of the hall while I searched the other side.

About five minutes later, Liam hissed, "I think I found it." He flashed his light to signal his position.

I rushed over and flashed my light over the dress. It was a strapless white satin dress with a sweetheart neckline with a sparkly waist clip. "This fits the description. Can you tell me if the gems are real?" I asked.

Liam pulled out a jeweler's loupe and, bending over, studied the clip. Shaking his head, he said, "They're paste. Very high quality, though. Very high."

Suddenly the room flooded with light.

Liam and I ducked down.

"What have we here?" floated Teddy's velvety voice. "Josiah, is that you?"

I stood up sheepishly.

"And you have a friend with you? Mind telling me what you think you're doing?"

"I'll be happy to explain if you'll put that gun down. I could ask you the same question. What are you doing here? Watching over your investment?"

Teddy did not lower his gun, but aimed it straight at us. "I don't think I need to explain anything to common burglars. I hate to do this, but I think I simply must call the police."

"Yeah, do that Teddy," I needled. "I'll be happy to explain to the police how you murdered both Bunny Witt and Emma Fisher."

Teddy slowly smiled, but I noticed his left eyebrow twitched when I said the word murder. "There goes that incredibly vivid imagination of yours again, Josiah."

"Madam, please shut up," cautioned Liam, who was standing beside me with his hands raised. "You're gonna get us killed."

"Why don't you listen to your friend? He has sense."

"Why aren't you calling the police, Teddy?" I challenged.

"Why would I have any reason to kill Bunny Witt or Emma Fisher?"

I stood beside the dress and pointed to the waist clip. "It was over this."

Teddy leaned his head back and let loose his best patrician laugh. "Those gems aren't real. That's junk paste."

"That's right. They are now, but they weren't paste when Bunny shipped the dress here, and they weren't paste when the dress was put on the mannequin. She told me she checked the dresses as soon as she landed from New York, and there was not a problem then. Only at the gala did Bunny realize something was amiss with this evening dress. She recognized that this clip was different. Perhaps she couldn't articulate the difference, but Bunny knew this was not the same clip that was originally shipped with the dress. She put two and two together and realized someone had made a replica and switched it with the genuine article. I think Bunny approached you on the night of the gala and made a big stink about it. Next thing you know, Bunny turns up dead."

"That's absurd," scoffed Teddy.

"Is it? I think when Bunny confronted you, you suggested that the two of you talk about it somewhere private."

"Like the carriage house? She wouldn't have gone there with me. I could never have convinced her to traipse down a gravel path to a dusty old shed."

"You convinced her, all right. You convinced her the way you manipulate so many women, by being a very smooth talker. You're good with women, and Bunny was a very naïve and vulnerable woman."

"Or maybe you convinced her with that pistol stuck in her back," chimed in Liam.

"You've no proof, just like you have no proof that I had anything to do with the death of Emma Fisher. I didn't even know the woman."

"But you did. Tell him what you worked out, Liam."

"While you were having tea with Lady Elsmere, I took the key from Emma Fisher's apartment that Madam had and compared it with the keys in your coat pocket. It matched a key from your key ring set. You were in possession of a key to Emma Fisher's apartment, and it's probably on your key ring right now. Very sloppy, mate," chided Liam.

Teddy's face suddenly glistened with perspiration.

I rambled on, "I've worked it all out, Teddy. You were

Emma's mystery boyfriend for over a year. It started when you read an interview with Bunny in a London paper. In the interview, Bunny talked about the fabulous jewels her great aunt received from her Indian lover and then hid where they remained undiscovered."

"You're saying I killed over some hearsay, rumors handed down from a daft old aunt," Teddy scoffed.

I continued, "The story fired your imagination. So you befriended poor Emma Fisher, a thirty-something woman with no sexual experience. You turned on the charm and seduced her. Emma was so enthralled with the attention, she couldn't say no. You talked her into giving you the London apartment's security codes, the door key, and had her draw a floor plan of Bunny's flat."

Liam took a tentative step.

Teddy, who responded by turning the gun squarely on him. "Don't even think it, chum," hissed Teddy.

I continued. "You couldn't find the gems, so you began stalking Bunny. When you tore up her London flat, she fled to New York, where you followed. You began pressuring Emma to get Bunny to change her will. You needed access to Bunny's estate and you needed to control Emma to get it."

Liam interrupted, "I've noticed you're not denying it, mate."

"Tell me, Josiah. How did you make the connection between the jewels and the exhibit?"

"That's simple. You still couldn't find the gems in the New York apartment, but you felt you could flush them out somehow by having this exhibit. There was never a

secret benefactor. It was just you all along. You must
have spent a small fortune making this happen."

"If Emma was so much under my thumb, why would
I have to kill her?"

"I think she became frightened after you murdered
Bunny. She knew you had to be the murderer, and you
were afraid she would talk. At the beginning of this
sordid tale, Emma was so in love with you, she wanted to
make you happy at all costs, but she never thought about
the consequences of having the will changed. It meant
Bunny had to die at some point, but when it finally
happened, it shocked Emma. After all, Bunny had been
good to her up to a point. Now Emma realized she was
an accomplice to murder, and that she might be next.
She stopped trusting you."

"This is a fantastic tale you've concocted. All
conjecture on your part. Poppycock," Teddy shot back.

I plowed on, "It wasn't until Theda Finkelstein related
to me Emma told her that she was 'being gaslighted' that
everything fell into place. I didn't have a clue what she
meant at first, but then it hit me. I realized exactly what
you were up to."

Teddy professed, "I don't understand."

"When someone is 'being gaslighted' they are slowly
being driven into madness or manipulated by a loved one.
It's a term inspired by the 1941 movie *Gaslight* with Ingrid
Bergman and Charles Boyer. It's about a jewel thief who
marries a young woman whose aunt hid her fabulous
jewels before her death. The husband tries to

drive his young wife insane while he searches for the jewels. Sound somewhat familiar to you?"

Teddy let out a haughty, condescending laugh. "Why would I kill this Emma person if she were the executrix of Bunny Witt's estate?"

"You had discovered the gems had been incorporated into the clip on this dress. You didn't need Emma any more. She was a loose end that needed to be tidied up. Emma simply knew too much."

"Kill her and let all that money from the estate slip through my fingers? That would be foolish," sneered Teddy, brandishing the gun again.

"But you were going to have your own fortune thanks to the gems you stole. Besides, real estate, stocks–those things don't interest you–don't excite you the way mysterious, long-lost jewels do."

Liam looked at me with genuine admiration. "Madam, very good. It's the lust for gems that makes a man a jewel thief. It's a lust that can be stronger than the desire for a woman."

"Speaking of women, let's move this discussion to me," I announced, slowly edging my way to the foyer.

"What about you, Josiah?"

"I kept wondering why someone like you would be showering me with attention, but it all became clear when we went to Lady Elsmere's for tea. You were using me to get close to June, so you could have access to her renowned jewelry collection. By dating me, you knew sooner or later you'd be invited to her mansion. You needed a new strategy after you botched the first attempt at burglary in the middle of the night. You weren't content with just Bunny's jewels. You wanted June's fabulous emerald necklace too. Somehow you drugged her on the night of her birthday party—not enough to knock her out but enough to muddle her mind.

"That's why Emma was so desperate to meet with me. She planned to warn me that you would be making a move on me, but lost her nerve."

"It was this sleeveen, Madam?" Liam put his hands down and made fists. "You're the bloody bastard who sneaked into the baby's room."

"I don't know Gaelic, but I doubt sleeveen was meant as a compliment," Teddy smirked. "Got the bedrooms mixed up. I would have retreated gracefully, but that bitch of a dog woke the entire house and chased me to the river. I had to give her a good swift kick to get away."

"You were trying to steal the Kaur emerald," I said.

"Yes, and why not? Don't you know about that necklace? The stones are some of the largest emeralds ever discovered, and were confiscated by the East India Company in 1705. The largest, the Kaur emerald, was sold to Lord Elsmere's family in 1784 by a Dutch diamond merchant, and has been in the family ever since then.

"The stone is priceless and that old crone was wearing

it to an afternoon tea in rural Kentucky with a bunch of her idiot friends. She doesn't deserve to have it."

"I'm something of a jewel fancier myself, Teddy boy, but I've never killed for them. You murdered two women for a bunch of rocks," spat Liam. "That's cold, mate. Very cold."

"Not to mention the fact that Teddy left you on the outs with Lady Elsmere and got you thrown out of the Big House," I added.

"Yeah, about that," growled Liam.

"Shut up. As for you, Josiah, you didn't get everything right, but close enough. Now I need you to move away from Danny Boy. Over by the door," commanded Teddy.

"Trying to make this look like a home invasion. It won't work," I insisted.

"I think it will. 'Officer, Josiah Reynolds and I were having an intimate moment in my quarters when I heard a noise downstairs. I investigated and she followed. When I turned on the lights, an armed intruder panicked and shot my lady friend. Naturally, I had to shoot him in self-defense.' That wasn't too difficult, was it? I almost convince myself. The police will have no trouble swallowing my story," Teddy crowed with sickening self-confidence.

Liam protested, "Sorry to disappoint, but I don't have a gun."

"You will by the time the police get here, and it will have your prints on it."

"I have a gun too, and it's trained at your head, Teddy!" In strolled Walter Neff aiming his Walther PPK squarely at Teddy. "Please make a move you limey bastard. I'd love to end this here with a bullet between your eyes."

I don't think I'll ever forget the look of astonishment on Teddy's face.

Liam walked over and calmly took Teddy's gun from his hand. "Cripes, lad, what took you so long?" Liam asked Walter.

Walter growled, "I wanted to hear this piece of scum confess to killing Bunny."

"He didn't deny it," pointed out Liam.

Walter replied, "Not good enough in a court of law, but he did state that he was going to kill you two."

Teddy shot a nasty look at me. "You set me up, you bitch."

I shrugged. "Aw, shucks. I can't take all the credit. Couldn't have done it without my homeboys, Walter and Liam."

"You've got nothing on me. I'll just say you made it up because I caught the three of you trying to steal these expensive dresses."

I explained, "The police might have gone for that if I hadn't taped our entire conversation. You're finished, Thaddeus McPherson, if that is your real name. I'm sure Interpol will identify you, but in any event, you'll rot in an American prison for the murders of Bunny and Emma. After all, you're in Kentucky and you'll face Kentucky justice." I walked over to him. "Were the gems worth all this pain and suffering? Where are they, Teddy? Where are the lost gems? Where is June's emerald necklace?"

"You'll never get your grubby hands on them, Josiah. Nobody will. Only I know the location of the gems. They are mine and no one else's."

"What good will they do you while you rot in a prison?" I asked, totally bewildered by this man's obsession.

Teddy began chortling and then laughing out loud. He didn't stop when the police came and handcuffed him. He was still laughing when the police car drove away.

He wouldn't tell the police where the gems were, not because he wouldn't, but because he couldn't. You see– Teddy had literally lost his mind. I'm not sure even he knows where they are anymore due to his deranged mind. He was so smugly sure of himself that Teddy couldn't cope when everything came unraveled.

No one knows where he hid Bunny's gems, and I don't think they ever will.

50

Goetz opened the door to his apartment and appeared genuinely surprised to see me. Pleasantly surprised? Time will tell. "What are you doing here?"

"I come bearing gifts," I replied, holding up a six-pack of beer. I pushed past him into the apartment.

"What do you want?"

"We're too damned old to fight and hold grudges. I'd be dead if it wasn't for you, so I've come to patch things up. I heard you have finally retired and thought you might want to celebrate."

Goetz grabbed a beer and pulled the tab. "You call this celebrating?"

"I've also ordered a pizza. Should be here in fifteen minutes, but you get to pay for it."

"Naturally. So we've got pizza and beer. Now what?"

"*Gaslight* is playing on TV tonight. Thought we should watch it, since it solved your murder cases for you–or I solved the murder cases for which you got credit. You're going out on top with your last two murder cases closed . . . thanks to whom?"

"Geez, Josiah, I've already thanked you. Enough's enough."

"Now you're retiring. All loose ends are sewn up. You're a free man, Goetz. The world is your oyster."

"I can't shake this case free. What makes a man so besotted with a diamond or a ruby that he'll kill two people over them and is willing to kill two more? It's baffling, and now I'm going to watch a movie about the same sickness. Tell me something. Do you think McPherson is insane or is he petending? And was it kismet that his path crossed those of Bunny and Emma?"

A quote from Shakespeare suddenly entered my mind. "Well, former Detective Goetz, a wise man once wrote, 'The fault, dear Brutus, is not in our stars, but in ourselves.'"

And with that I clicked on the TV.

51

Walter Neff hid in the bushes until the newly employed night watchman at Hilltop Manor made his last rounds and headed for his car in the parking lot, where he could listen to a West Coast baseball game and eat his baloney sandwich in peace.

Walter's legs were stiff from crouching in hiding for long hours, waiting until all the other employees left. He was also sweating profusely, and felt clammy which Walter attributed to his long wait. He had come in with the last tour of the day and veered off, hoping they would not notice his absence. It had worked.

Now Walter had Hilltop Manor to himself. He hurried to the back rose garden, where a rope hung over the brick wall. Tugging on it, Walter pulled over a backpack filled with equipment he would need.

From the backpack, Walter took out a metal detector, a short folding shovel, night goggles, a garden trowel, and another little bag. He had been practicing all week with his new metal detector, and felt confident he knew how to use it correctly.

Walter had been putting the pieces together since Teddy's incarceration. He believed with his whole heart that Teddy's current bout of insanity was a façade, and if he ever won a reprieve from the courts, Teddy would make a beeline for Hilltop Manor.

The gems had to be somewhere on the property. Where else could Teddy have hidden them? The very fact that he was staying at Hilltop Manor instead of a nice, cushy hotel, proved to Walter that Teddy was guarding the clip and the emerald necklace somewhere in the vicinity. He was pretty sure Teddy had neither the time nor the opportunity to dismantle the gold clip and stash the gems elsewhere. It had to be intact. His guess was that Teddy had buried it somewhere on the property.

Walter put on his night goggles and pulled out a map of the property he had snatched the night Bunny went missing. Unfolding it, he studied it carefully, as he had every night since Teddy had been taken into custody. He would start with the old tobacco barn in the north pasture. Walter figured since Teddy was a city person, he must have hidden the gems in a building. City people tended to use buildings as a frame of reference rather than fences or trees as they were unfamiliar with hiding things there, which a country resident would be more likely to do.

Walter spent over an hour in the old barn, finding nothing but rusty nails and tabs of soda cans. Wiping his sweaty brow with a faded hankie, Walter leaned against a post, trying to think like Teddy. Since Teddy had been staying in a back bedroom, it would have made sense to pick a hiding place he could see from his window.

As much as Walter disliked getting close to the mansion, due to the presence of the new guard, Walter felt he had no choice. He crept closer to the house, keeping an eye out for the watchman. Peering through the wrought iron gate, Walter could see the guard had fallen asleep in his car with a baseball game blaring on the radio.

It was now or never. Walter might not get another chance.

Standing under the window of the room Teddy had stayed in, Walter surveyed the grounds. As far as he could tell, nothing looked out of place.

There was a shade garden filled with hostas under a massive white oak tree and then there was the perennial garden with a beehive. Beyond that was an orchard.

Walter's gaze locked onto the beehive–the perfect hiding place. Most people would never go near it for fear of being stung. Since it was not yet harvest time, the beekeeper would not open the hive for some months yet.

Remembering that at night all the bees were inside the hive and calm, Walter figured as long as he did not bump the hive, make noise, or shine a light inside the hive, the bees would remain passive. That much he had learned from Josiah.

Walter carefully approached the hive from the back. He was afraid of honeybees, however, the desire to find the clip was stronger than his fear.

He turned on the metal detector and approached the hive. Even though the device made a low, humming noise, the bees did not come out to investigate. Walter slowly moved around the hive until he made a complete circle. As soon as he moved the detector's coil under the hive, a strong clicking alarm sounded, indicating it had found something.

Marking the spot, Walter turned off the metal detector. He then noted another humming sound that he had hoped he wouldn't hear.

The honeybees were aware that something was outside their hive, and were rousing the guard bees to take a peek.

Breaking out in a sweat, Walter dropped to his hands and knees, reached into the space beneath the hive and scraped away dirt with his trowel. He knew it couldn't be too deep. Teddy would have to be able to grab the gems at a moment's notice.

He had barely begun when the blade of the trowel struck something. Walter cast the trowel aside, and reaching his arm under the hive bottom, he poked around in the dirt until he felt a canvas sack. In his excitement, Walter grabbed the sack and got up too quickly, accidentally knocking over the hive.

Thousands of enraged honeybees spilled out of the toppled hive, looking for something to punish for damaging their home.

Walter ran like Old Scratch was after him on a full-moon-lit night, trying to snatch his soul.

After about a hundred feet or so, the number of bees chasing Walter dwindled to a few. He had been stung multiple times on his hands, arms, and face, but the adrenaline of finding the canvas sack made Walter oblivious to the pain.

He slowed to a walk, but was still breathing hard when he found a bench to sit down. Carefully Walter untied the filthy red canvas bag and shook out its contents. There in his hand, glistening in the Kentucky moonlight, was the gold clip with the gems intact. Bunny's aunt had fashioned the clip years ago to hide the gems on her dress in plain sight. Her plan had been pure genius.

Clasping his chest, Walter gasped, "I finally hit the jackpot! I found them! I found them, Bunny!" He shook the bag again, and out fell Lady Elsmere's emerald necklace.

Walter was still rejoicing in his good fortune when he collapsed on the ground, gripping the clip with one hand and his chest with the other.

Poor Walter.

He didn't realize he was having a heart attack. As he pulled off the night goggles, he murmured, "Oh, God, what's happening to me?"

No one was there to respond. Only the sound of his voice drifted on a gentle breeze up to the treetops, and blended in with the mournful howl at the moon from a lonely dog in the distance.

52

I read in the paper that Walter Neff had suffered a severe heart attack and had been discovered beneath some bushes in one of the Hilltop Manor gardens. The person who called 911 did not identify himself, nor could the police trace the call.

In addition to the heart attack, Walter had sustained numerous bee stings, two broken fingers, which the doctor assumed occurred when he fell, but he couldn't explain why the EMTs had found Walter with his hoodie unzipped, his belt unbuckled, and lying prone on his back as if someone had been performing CPR on him.

Next to Walter were a pair of night goggles and an empty red canvas bag. Nothing else of value was discovered.

The newspaper article did not offer an explanation as

to why Walter Neff might have been prowling Hilltop Manor's grounds. The article closed by stating that Walter was conscious, but still expected to remain in ICU for some time.

I put down the paper and called Goetz, but he said he couldn't tell me anything, reminding me that since he had retired, he was out of the loop.

I knew he was lying, but decided not to press the issue.

Walter had no kin, so I knew I should probably be the one to check on him–not that I wanted to do so. Walter was a pain in the tuckus, but he was alone and down on his luck. I also wanted to ask him about the red canvas bag.

The police might not have a clue why Walter was rooting around the grounds of Hilltop Manor, but I did. Reading between the lines of the newspaper story, I guessed Walter might have found the jewels, but apparently hid them before his heart attack. Or maybe . . . hmm, something else occurred . . ."

Sometimes my brain does work, and I can fit the pieces of the puzzle together. So Walter was found prone, like someone had been performing CPR.

Whom did I know who was sneaky and capable of following Walter without being detected, and also loved jewels?

I jumped up from my chair. "LIAM! LIAM! I NEED TO HAVE A LITTLE TALK WITH YOU!

53

Liam didn't hear Josiah yell for him. He was on a plane to Europe.

"Would you like a glass of champagne, sir?" asked the solicitous first class flight attendant.

"Yes, I would," replied Liam. He accepted the champagne and, before taking a sip, Liam looked out the window and saluted. "Thanks, Walter. I couldn't have done it without you."

In a few hours, Lady Elsmere, aka June Webster of Monkey's Eyebrow, would awake to find her emerald necklace on the pillow beside her, and Josiah Reynolds would find a packet for Walter Neff in her mailbox. It contained one deep red ruby, enough to pay his medical bills and more.

Smiling, Liam settled in his comfy chair, very pleased with himself. Yes, very pleased, indeed.

CPSIA information can be obtained
at www.ICGtesting.com
Printed in the USA
LVOW11s0147261116
514516LV00001B/29/P